Dear D[...] [...]t
you a[...]
special sistah!
Cheers to
the bubbly!

This book is a result of my enriching eight years in the
Democratic Republic of Congo. I am grateful to the most
fantastic story tellers I met, the country and people.

With best wishes

Astha Singh

ACCRA,

Congo

A Journey

Astha Singh

ZORBA BOOKS

Published in India by Zorba Books, 2015

Website: www.zorbabooks.com
Email: info@zorbabooks.com

Copyright © Astha Singh

ISBN 978-93-85020-21-6

All rights reserved. No part of this book may be reproduced or transmitted
in any form or by any means, electronic or mechanical, including
photocopying, recording, or by an information storage and retrieval
system—except by a reviewer who may quote brief passages in a review to
be printed in a magazine, newspaper, or on the Web—without permission in
writing from the copyright owner.

Although the author and publisher have made every effort to ensure the
accuracy and completeness of information contained in this book, we
assume no responsibility for errors, inaccuracies, omissions, or any
inconsistencies herein. Any slights on people, places, or organizations are
unintentional.

Zorba Books Pvt. Ltd. (opc)
Gurgaon, INDIA

Cover design by Qualcom Design

Printed in India

PROLOGUE

3-1-2014
Avenue de Fleur, Gombe, Kinshasa.
Democratic Republic of Congo.
Time : 3:00 a.m.

She was sprawled out on his red and gold, crystal-studded velvet bed. The air conditioner and the generator were wheezing in tandem. The tall, red and gold lamps in the room cast long shadows on the thick gold satin curtain.

'*Eh toi*! Stop pulling my bra. *Ca coute tres cher*. Very expensive, *tu vois*,' she said, as she batted her very long, dense and false eyelashes. She had spent a fortune on those lashes. They were pink and black with a splash of gold glitter, in the latest club-style fashion. She lazily twirled a thick strand of her fake Brazilian blonde hair around her index finger. Her lips formed a perfect chocolate brown sulky pout – she now knew that was enough to melt a man's heart, and loosen his purse and zipper for sure.

'*Cherie*, I buy you plenty like this in *couler rouge*! Plenty, plenty. You no have enough place to keep all the bra and painty I buy you.' He grinned, displaying the bitter cola bits stubbornly stuck on his yellow teeth. He raised his index finger to his mouth and picked out a few bits of bitter cola from his teeth, stared at and then snapped and flicked it out. The chewed bits of bitter cola landed on the latest fancy remote control. He picked it up, did not bother with his spit and switched on the music system. Nonchalance is the style of the rich, he knew.

The iPod played songs by Musique System, a well-known band from Ivory Coast. The trendy night-clubs played all their songs.

'*Premier gao ne pas gao...* aaoo... aaoo... aaoo,' he crooned along, while ripping the clothes off her. There was a sense of urgency for he had popped a Viagra. The magic pill that Suraj Deshpande, his entertainment manager had got for him from Mumbai.

'Ohhh... It is too much danger pill. The ministers love it, the big officers at the port love it, and the Juju man loves it! *Pappa*, I don't have time for such thoughts. I am a businessman and I want total value for money.'

'Make full use of Viagra, the sex pill. *Patron*! Rum-pum-pum all night boss! The pill is like you. On fire!' Suraj had said to him. He shook his head to change his thoughts. Time was running out and he had to hurry. He pinned her down and made love to her like never before. He was the savage hungry hunter and she his prey. He had to leave his mark all over her body, and claim her completely. She was his personal conquest. He had watched many porn CDs during his free time in his early days, and tried to emulate the exact moves. It was difficult initially, but now with enough practice it worked!

"This hot girl, my latest girlfriend all of seventeen had actually been dating my eldest son till last month. But, guess what? She is my girlfriend now. I can have what I want... even my son's girlfriend!" He laughed.

He remembered with excitement, how he first spotted her at Club VIP, the popular night club on *Boulevard du 30 Juin.* It was a few weeks before Christmas and Club VIP as usual, was bustling with United Nations men who could never get enough of Congolese nightlife.

'These people don't know how to party. Bloody desperate men. They come to Congo on a contract for one year, and want to have the time of their lives. I don't give a fuck to these men,' Seth Manikchand said to his assistant. He was now in the big boys' league. The big bad boys who walked in late, their tables reserved, were served by their usual waiters. He entered Club VIP with some of his new friends, and waited at the bar for the club manager to organize his spot.

'*Patron,* have a drink and I make you a place,' said, the young manager. '*Pas de* problem, chief! Tonight you are *plein*. Full, eh! *Becoupe de noveau femme*. But, me? I no like any of your girls. Bring new sexy ones or I go to Club Belize,' Manikchand joked with the manager.

'*Patron*, you deserve girls from Moulin Rouge, Paris. These girls are not your level,' responded the manager. Manikchand loved being pampered.

He laughed, '*C'est vrais*!' His eyes had adjusted to the dark interiors of the club and he was enjoying the music. The waiter fixed his usual drink and handed it to him. He took a long slug of his Black Label on ice, and enjoyed the golden liquid go down the throat into his belly. It felt good. He loved his first long gulp; it never failed to make him happy. He was ready for Friday night.

The dance floor was packed with people, dancing with passion. 'It's funny how language becomes meaningless when the music is good. All these Indian *chokra log* don't understand a word of French, and look at their dancing. *Saala*, they shake their heads as if they were born listening to French songs,' he thought to himself and laughed. He was reminded of his first visit to a nightclub in Bujumbura; and how gawky and unsure he was. The first flush and flurry of witnessing exposed breasts and close dancing with strange women. He was snapped out of his thoughts when he suddenly spotted his eldest son on the dance floor. He leaned over to check out the girl his son was dancing with, and his jaw dropped.

'*Arrey saala*, the bloody son of a bitch is dancing with such a bombshell. *Ekdum item che,* boss!' He slapped his right thigh and laughed.

'What a sexy girl, but completely wasted on my useless son,' he thought. She was close dancing with his twenty-year-old 'always sulking and useless' son. Her lithe body was wrapped around his son. He shamelessly stared at her tiny waist and that big protruding round butt, moving in perfect rhythm to the beat of the music. '*Aicha, ecoute moi...comme ci...je ne existe pas,*' the DJ belted the remixed version of the old popular French classic, '*Aicha*'.

It was now past midnight in Kinshasa, and the energy was high on the dance floor like always. The 'Night Queens' were working on their moves, trying to solicit clients. Each girl trying hard to be better than the other, their well-rounded curvaceous bodies rocking to the beat of music. But, she – the girl dancing with his son, stood out. He could tell that most men at the club had their eyes on her. She was fresh and different. The fog machine kept coughing up smoke and the haze made her appear even more alluring. The thick cigar smoke and an intense mélange of different perfumes and after shaves. The atmosphere was charged with raw sex appeal. She was unaware of the number of eyeballs on her. Her body moved to the music, she was born to dance. As the music reached a crescendo, she started shaking her hips like an experienced belly dancer. He was reminded of his dream girl, Parveen Babi, the Bollywood dancing sensation in the 1970s. She looked absolutely divine under the multi-colour halo of the shiny disco light. The tight fitted off-shoulder black and gold dress accentuated her waist and restrained her breasts that were ready to pop out from the extra tight outfit. She had sprinkled gold glitter on her breasts and it reflected under the strobe lights. He was bedazzled.

The attendant had to actually scream into his ears, '*Patron, votre table est pret.*' His usual spot in the club was arranged. He always sat next to the bar, right at the edge of the dance floor. The leather couches were comfortable; it provided an excellent view of the dance floor; and it was easy to get catch the bartender's eye for quick refills. He rushed to recline on his favourite brown leather couch, trying to suppress a massive erection.

'Ripe, ready and juicy. *Saala*, I need her. She is a ripe Alphonso mango. I have to have her,' he said to no one in particular. Anyway, no one paid attention to what people say in Club VIP. It was a place meant for pleasure. He knew he needed her, his body was rebelling, and his groin was throbbing. His hand moved to his zipper and he tried to press his hard-on down. He opened a new sachet of *gutkha*, and dropped the entire content in his mouth. He was chewing hard and fast, his right foot was tapping with the music. He was thinking hard. He needed her. He wanted her. She was meant for him and his body. Like a true connoisseur of luxury items, he lazily appraised her.

'When I see a diamond, I instantly know the value.'– his companion tonight, the old Greek man – wasn't paying any attention to what he was saying. He absently nodded or smiled.

'My ancestors were jewellers, you see!' He told the old Greek coffee trader, who was busy smoking his cigar and watching the girls on the dance floor. Manikchand was paying their bill tonight. He had rented the Greek man's sprawling villa in Gombe to run a Mumbai style dance bar. The bar girls came very cheap and no one had ever thought of opening one in Kinshasa.

The girl dancing with his son was beautiful, is an understatement. He was desperate for her and he wanted her now. He called out to the one of the waitresses.

'*Ma belle*, who is that young *Metisse* girl dancing with the Indian boy there?' he asked her. The music was too loud for them to have a conversation. She kept his double shot of Black Label on the table, and leaned forward to scream into his ear. He enjoyed the full front view of her breasts. They had many stretch marks, he noticed; she was wearing a pink and purple bra.

'*Quoi*?' she yelled, over the music. He grabbed her left arm with his right hand and pulled her closer to him. He regretted immediately, her breath reeked of garlic and rotten fish. He held his breath and screamed into her ears.

'Who is that girl?' he asked, as he stared at the girl dancing with his son. He pointed in her direction and said, '*La bas, regarde,* the beautiful girl, *la bas*.'

The waitress understood instantly, many men were enquiring about that girl. But, the new girl wasn't available, since she hadn't informed the waiters that she was soliciting customers. She usually came in with a bunch of young girls and boys. The waitress sighed and adjusted her bra strap, before kneeling down to speak to Manikchand.

'Oh… *Elle est Charlotte. Tres complique, cette fills la*. Sometimes she says her father was an impoverished Belgian professor and mother, a rich Congolese heiress. But, sometimes she also says her father was Lebanese and very rich and her mother, a struggling Congolese painter. God alone knows who she really is. She is here with her friends often, *Patron.*' He slipped a five-dollar bill into her sweaty palms.

He couldn't take his eyes off her. Charlotte was born to stand out. She could easily be mistaken for a model or a

Nollywood star. In fact better than any Nigerian heroines he knew. She was short and curvaceous. Her sharp, chiseled nose was a bit upturned, making her appear arrogant. A pair of wide set, big watery eyes and high cheekbones. She would press and pout her lips often. Charlotte was the latest debutante in the nightclub circuit. 'She is new and she is fresh. She has to be mine. Money can buy anything, *Boni Patron.*' He reminded himself, and laughed. 'How difficult will it be to move this smoldering hot girl away from my son's arms and his second hand Toyota Corolla car, and into my bed – right under my perfumed body?' he wondered.

'Its all about money… *L'argent… Paisa,*' he just knew. He touched the black amulet coiled around his neck, it was the power centre of energy. He rubbed his finger against the soft red fabric and felt the magic bone wrapped within, it had real power and he felt reassured.

'*Merci beaucoup*, Matondo,' he murmured.

Seth Manikchand must be forty five or fifty years old. Anyway who cares how old you are? How much you weigh? What matters in this city of West Africa is how much money you have. It doesn't matter what you do? How you do? It is how much money you have? '*Comme bien de l'argent*?' *Khallas*. It is all about your net worth. He doesn't know his birthday or year, but celebrates it whenever he wants.

'The advantage of no specific birthday? It can be celebrated any day or any time of the year. *Saala*, I am a *pucca harami*, I can have plenty birthday parties in one year. Who cares? If there is enough *daru* in the bar and some *masala* entertainment! No one counts the years!' He laughed.

In his remote village in Kutch (Gujarat, India) they remembered a child's birth by rainfall, a drought or a calamity in the family. His mother would often recall with horror that three important members from their community died on the day he was born, and that their village suffered a huge drought. She would often curse the planet he was born under. 'It was an inauspicious planet. It ruined his mind and character,' she would mutter under her breath, each time she saw him.

How does it matter now? Manikchand was in his late forties or early fifties, 5 feet 8 inches tall, slight built, and had a small protruding belly. His physique was that of a man who didn't exercise, but enjoyed his meals and beer. He had lanky arms and legs and a young exuberant body. He had his mother's skin, tan yet not very dark. But it was ravaged by chicken pox marks. That was the first thing anybody would notice about his face, the pock-marks. The goddess had unleashed her fury on his face – at least that's what they said in his village. '*Devi nu prakop che...*' He had the curse written all over his face.

He constantly chewed *gutkha* and always carried toothpicks in his pocket to pick at his teeth. Sometimes, while working late into the night, bitter cola replaced the *gutkha*. It gave him the energy to stay awake and alert while working. He had the advantage of being an average man, not too tall and not too short; not fat and not thin; not good looking, but not ugly either. He could easily camouflage in a crowd.

He lay naked next to Charlotte, exhausted and spent. She was sipping a chilled bottle of Mutzig beer and was rubbing his slight paunch, while he panted. His chest, had no hair and he was proud of it. His favourite Bollywood star, Salman Khan flaunted a hairless chest. He would always say, 'I am like Salman *bhai*, *ekdum chikna ekdum mast*. *Bindass*! Just like *bhai*!'

'Charlotte, *ma cherie*, one day we go to Mumbai. You and me. We stay in Taj hotel and party with Bollywood stars. I will take you to meet big Bollywood producers. You can do one item number. *Ekdum DHANSOO*. *Ekdum* different. No one has thought of an African beauty dancing in Bollywood movies. You see, me? I think different!' He laughed and crushed her in an embrace.

'*Cherie*, I adore your bed. I always want to sleep on it. Promise me, *mon coeur*.' She purred and pounced like a kitten to kiss him on the lips. He held her tight. She was giggling and trying to wriggle out. He let go off her.

'*Allez*! *Kende*! Go where you want to. But no man will spend money on you like I do.' He pretended to look upset.

'Ohhh, my baby. I love you with all my body and heart,' she responded, as she leaned forward like a seductive dancer. She placed one leg on the side table and caressed her leg. She pouted and said, 'I will be back,' in a husky voice, and slowly walked to the bathroom. She stopped at the door, turned around and laughed. 'I will shower and be right back darling. Be ready, I will crush you when I come back.' Charlotte tightly wrapped her expensive hair in a bun, and pulled out a plastic shower cap from her bag. She had to protect her new natural hair from Brazil. He could hear her singing aloud in the bathtub.

Charlotte shouted from the bathroom, 'Darling, keep the bed ready. *J'arrive*! I am coming. I can't leave this bed. I love it. I feel like a princess in it!' He was smiling. He was proud of his bed.

It was a massive red leather bed studded with crystals, imported from Indonesia. He moved to this house a year ago. He had heard somewhere, at a posh party of the rich, well connected and well-traveled expats, that Indonesia produced the best furniture. He ordered a container of luxurious, Bollywood style furniture through his new Sindhi friend *toute suite*. Jimmy Biyani imported the best high-end furniture from South East Asia; and also had an atelier where he manufactured custom made exotic African furniture, to cater to the expats. He supplied imported furniture to top local people, and local Congolese handicrafts and furniture to the *Mundeles* – the expats. Now he could afford the best of everything. He had the money and he could always buy style and class.

He called up Jimmy Biyani, '*Bhai*, I want to furnish my new villa. You know *na*; I buy a new villa on *Avenue de Fleur*, near *Cercle Francais*. Furniture should be *ekdum jalsa* type. *Comme la* magazine. Like the *patron log* in big villas. You see some Bollywood magazines. *Tres chic*. Money no problem, but the furniture should be top class. I no have time. Once renovation done, I move in.'

Jimmy Biyani completely understood Manikchand's requirement and delivered the furniture in a month's time. His container full of bling-bling over the top furniture was the talk of the town. Society wives 'tsked tsked' his classless tacky choices but secretly wanted to have a peek. The rich business class made a joke out of it, though they were envious and outraged at the audacity of a common man who was now pushing all limits. The lower and middle class, working expats, saw this as an aspirational success story and looked up to him. After all he was one of them and if he could make it big, who knows? Some day they can start off on their own and make mega money. Everyone in the town was talking about Seth Manikchand, the new eccentric '*Patron*' in town.

'Time flies.' He couldn't believe that he had already spent a year and a half in this swanky up-market house. He hosted parties, entertained all kinds of businessmen, smugglers, politicians, musicians and bar dancers from Mumbai. The house was meant for a good life.

This luxurious imported bed was meant for a few, extremely pretty girls; the other regular girls were entertained in the other bedrooms. He had brought many in to this exclusive bed, but none was quite like Charlotte. She was his conquest now! As Charlotte emerged from the bathroom, he threw a brand new iPhone in her direction.

'*Mamma Ngai!*' she squealed, with joy. She quickly opened the packaging and started assembling the phone; while he lazily nuzzled and caressed her all over with his *gutkha* pouch, *Rajnigandha*, fresh from India.

Charlotte, all of seventeen, was a beautiful *metisse*. *Cafe au lait* skin, big breasts, unused and untouched by the world and big pouty lips. He did not want to forget that she was sleeping with his son just a few days ago. 'I now have the power to bring anyone into my bed. ANYONE! A young handsome man even?' he asked himself, and chuckled at the thought. He couldn't help snapping his fingers in excitement. His mind was working overtime, it always did.

'*Saala*, I am so *harami*. How would it feel to screw one of those English – French speaking wives of the stuck-up, university returned, *paisawala* bastards? The society ladies, with their stiff coiffed hair and French manicures; and that look of constant disdain on their faces. I hate their facial expression, always looking down on people, always exasperated... always so full of complain. They are never happy; always annoyed with something that is not important. I need to have some of them here in my bed. The rich bitches. They need to be taught a lesson. I will make them beg for mercy. Beg for forgiveness for their years of arrogance. I will spit on their pricey pussies in the end. I will spit on the false big fake boobs that they repair and enhance year after year. I will have to give them a fuck', he whispered to himself.

He gently stroked his inner thigh and was thinking to himself whose wife could be an easy prey. He laughed. These days he did that a lot. He felt proud of his achievement and laughed at his own thoughts and jokes. He often spoke to himself.

'Money does that to you. It makes you intelligent.' He laughed again. His mind was racing now, as he tried to decide which society wife to target.

'It will be an exciting game.' He rubbed his hands in glee.

'I love challenges. Who wants an easy lay, *yaar*? I will hunt down the extreme socialite. The most arrogant bitch among them all. How I would love to see her moan in my bed. I will ruffle her permanently coiffed hair, and scratch her naked body. She will lie naked and exposed in front of me.' He was enjoying these delicious thoughts. He had finally figured out the big secret. He would always wonder about the sudden growth of perky breasts in women. He also wanted to know why most of the rich women looked very surprised all the time. He now knew that the surprised expression on their faces and tight big breasts were all magic surgery. He watched Dr. 90210 on TV with much delight.

'Things money can buy? *Kamal che*! Beauty and youth even? It's important to create wealth *bhai*, or you can't live in this world.' He enjoyed his thoughts.

'All that business class tickets these rich women bought, to fly to Johannesburg, Dubai and Beirut for 'repair and maintenance' of their youth. And they never allow their husbands to touch them. The women don't want to spoil their assets.' All this was fresh information, which his new girlfriends would give him. He was enjoying their complicated society. He loved the web of intrigues in the rich world. It almost read like the stories in gossip magazines. Most men anyway were busy screwing other women or toy boys, so they didn't really care about the eccentricities of their wives. He found the idea of taking young men as lovers disgusting and abhorring. He would never ever do something like that. 'What is so exciting about a young man?' he wondered. The rich and powerful with their manicured hands enjoyed the company of young *mundele* NGO men; and, showered them with wine, *moules-frites* and gifts. They enjoyed lavish weekends, splashing in the pools of their fortified villas.

He remembered one rich man's words, 'The wives should be kept busy with pregnancy and partying!' The rich men would always laugh at such jokes. He loved how men with money got away with everything. No one questioned their morals and methods. He was almost there, and he was working on acquiring the mannerisms of the rich.

'I love it, *mon couer,*' Charlotte said, as she pouted her lips, while playing with the new I phone. He loved her French accent. It was very sexy.

'*Merci beaucoup.* I can't wait to click pictures and listen to songs on *mon noveau* phone.' She sprawled on his massive bed, admiring the new phone. And suddenly like a tigress, she jumped and got on her knees. He was enjoying her seductress act. She looked at the big silver framed mirror across the bed, held her phone at an angle, tilted her head, formed a perfect pout and clicked herself.

'Oohh… *Tres belle… Tres belle.*' He grabbed her by her fake blonde hair and pulled her close. He kissed her full on her mouth and clicked her picture with his phone.

'*Cherie*, put it on Facebook. Ha, ha, ha... Let Kinshasa witness our love,' he said.

'Oh, *mon coeur*, they will be too much jealous,' she replied.

'Upload it now, *Cherie*, from your new iPhone. Now,' he said. She did what he asked for and voila! 'Beep, Beep, Beep,' went her new phone.

'*Mon Couer*, plenty people are liking our pictures but no comments. They are too jealous. I told you, this town is full of haters,' she said and pretended to sulk. He knew what he was doing. The Bose sound system in his room played her favourite songs on a loop.

'Manikchand! *Kaminey*! You motherfucker! You son of a whore! "Come out… come out if have guts…" Where the fuck are you, you fuck face *chodu*?' screamed a young man downstairs.

'No, no… *Arret toi. C'est qui, la*?' the cook was heard shouting back. Someone banged open the sitting room door and flung a chair downstairs. An expensive crystal vase from China came crashing down. Another made in China vase was flung from across the table. The red and yellow plastic flowers lay scattered on the floor.

'Ai, ai, ai… *Michel, Kanga port*,' Manikchand yelled. He got up, pulled on his new red silk pajamas and red silk robe; and came running down the stairs of his double storey house.

'*Guardian*, what is the noise? Who is shouting? Is this why I pay you lazy buggers so that I no rest in peace? Who is it?' Manikchand bellowed, as he ran downstairs. The other staff from the servant's quarter came scurrying down into the living room. '*C'est moi, pappa*. It's me your son!' slurred the unsteady Sameer. His body reeked of alcohol and his eyes were bloodshot red, as if he had been crying. He brandished a pistol; his hands were unsteady.

'No, Sam. No, *arret toi. Calm toi.*' The old *Papa* Andre grabbed his arms and hissed into his ears, '*Arret...* Now, now. You stop. *Sam, arret toi, yaka. Mamma ngaai.* Saaaaam *arret, mobulu toi*,' begged the old retainer.

Michel ran out from the kitchen. Michel was the same age as Sameer, and worked as a houseboy at Manikchand's Villa.

'*Mon ami, c'est que ca*? Calm *toi,* Sammy. I get you chilled Coca,' he said, and dashed into the kitchen; and ran out breathless holding a chilled Coke can.

'You will pay for this, you motherfucker Ramesh. You will pay for your sins. The Lord is too kind to you, but I am not. My mother has cried many nights because of you, bastard! I will kill you,' Sameer yelled again. He grabbed the Coke can, snapped it open and chugged it. Manikchand was in the salon.

'Samu, *su che*? Why you create a *hangama*? You want money, my *dikro* my son? I give you money tomorrow. Now go home,' Manikchand said.

'*Harami saala. Zoba,*' Sameer yelled, as he picked up a little side table with his left hand and flung it at Manikchand.

'Pappa, I hate you. Pappa, I hate you,' he sobbed. Manikchand tilted to his left to avoid the being hit by the table. Sameer held the pistol with both his hands.

'Don't move or I shoot all of you.' Sameer was reeking of alcohol and weed.

'Don't move,' he shouted again. 'I will shoot you!'

CONTENTS

Manikchand Seth… Range Rover and Single Malt

Manikchand Seth was the new millionaire on the block, and he was living it up. People called him *"patron de patron"*, *"boss de boss"*, *"vrais patron"*, and *"boni patron"*.

'I love being the *patron*. The Boss!' He smiled that smile of glee, cunning and satisfaction, exposing his *gutkha* stained teeth. He had never been happier. Now was his moment. He was loving it, and living it. He felt like an old Russian airplane that has made a successful landing, woosh… on the legendary Kinshasa tarmac. The long, tedious and even dangerous flight, forgotten under the thunderous claps and cries of *'Dans mon pays! Dans mon Pays!'* The unadulterated joy of making it despite all odds.

'Ha! Ha! Ha! Who is having the last laugh? Now, I will show those bastards, the old money bastards what it means to have *paisa? Arreey saala!* Look how they open their shiny gold-knobbed doors, and lay out their best china for me. Now, they all come to me for personal favours,' he thought to himself – he was ecstatic.

'Seth, ministry mein kaam hai', *'Seth, port par kuch lafda hai'*, *'Douane* pe container *phansa hai'*, 'Seth, please set up a meeting for me with the new minister' – and he with an imperial sweep of his hand would proclaim, *'Problem nathi'*, 'No problem', *'Cava allez'*. 'You have to speak a bit of French to show class', he told himself. "No more Lingala. No *'Papa Yaka. Pesa Mai'*. *'Kanga port'* Gujrati, nathi … sala … No … NO NO … *Jamais. No more Bande Rouge moko…* say *'Amenez moi* Glen, double!'" Though, honestly he preferred chilled Mutzig over any of these fancy Single Malts. 'But, what to do *saala*?! I have to gulp this malt and that malt down

for these bloody motherfuckers – to show that I'm in their league, and even better placed than most of them, in all of Congo.' He thought.

Now, the rich and elite of Congo – 'they' wanted to be invited to his decadent parties. 'They' laughed at his crude jokes, and admired his 4.5 carat diamond ring and his fine Rolex watch.

His spanking new, shiny black Range Rover was the talk of Kinshasa town. He maintained it like his new girlfriend. He had heard somewhere that, 'Your *ladki* and *gaadi* should be *chakmak* – maintain your girl and your car.' He hunted down the alleys of *Bon Marche*, an area largely dominated by the Lebanese community to refurbish his car. Bon Marche was the best place to buy expensive and unique car accessories.

'Oh! The Lebanese people know how to live. *Mast shinney* cars and *gori chitti biwi*. When I visit them, I can't take my eyes off their women. What white arms? Just like a slab of marble. The Lebanese women are like Taj Mahal. White, shiny and beautiful. Have you seen their lips? Big juicy, like a ripe strawberry. You want to bite and lick the juice that drips off. But no *bhai*. Don't even think... *Jamais*! The Lebanese men? They are too danger. Hot head and hawk eyes. You look at their women and their blood will boil. No more *dhanda* with you. *C'est finis Alor*! And soon you will be deported. Very well connected, they are. Anyway, my hands are full,' he would tell all.

'You should see this Lebanese owned shop, *Car Jazz*. It's like Diwali *dhamaka*! I was dazzled and asked the old owner's son to tip top my car. I clearly told him, *Mon ami! Toi!* You think that this is your car and you are sexing it up to impress your girlfriend. Money no issue. Do it top of the line. Total fit fat. *Ekdum* superfine. *Commes les Arabs*!' Manikchand loved to flaunt.

And the Range Rover was embellished with the latest trappings – Black leather seats, a top of the range sound system and his favourite air purifier. ''Ambience is important!'' he declared to no one in particular. These days he was getting smart thoughts and he liked to share it with everyone, and people did stop to listen. When money talks, no one checks the grammar. Sometimes, from among his audience, usually a rich man would call out to his other rich friends and ask him to repeat the wise words. And together they would laugh. 'Dude, tell us a joke, *yaar*.' Manikchand enjoyed such attention.

'Let me tell you, when I was flying business class to Dubai, I call the airhostess. What your name? I ask her. "Eva Benz," she say to me. "You cousin of Mercedes Benz?" I ask. "Maintenance cost is same," she said. *Saali. Too much chalu cheeze*.' They laughed. He loved it.

He felt 'arrived' in the company of these rich men with their designer outfits, shoes and limited edition watches. But somehow he still always felt small. He really tried hard to belong, yet he still felt like an outsider. He couldn't break into their rarefied, exclusive circle. The cigar smoking, holidaying in the South of France, they owned villas in European cities. Most had attended elementary school at the American, Belgian and French International Schools; before moving to Europe, America and Canada for further education.

He always told them, 'You people are the 5 star, first class, *ekdum* magazine types of Indians. So much style, Boss! You are like film stars in everything you do and even in how you do. The way you eat that tasteless limp sushi with two thin sticks. How you eat the spaghetti with a fork while rolling it on a spoon, it's an art. How you also manage to have soup without making any sound? It is really tiring to spend time with you. Your parents were friends, turned business rivals, turned friends, and then rivals again. Very complicated boss.'

'Ekta Kapoor will make so much money. If only she visited West Africa once. The Indians here do more drama than Indians anywhere else in the world,' Manikchand would always tell his friends. 'Especially all the very fine *bhabhi jis*, they are too much *nautanki*. They can also act in all the Zee TV and Sony TV serials that they watch all the time.'

Manikchand got smart ideas now, and he enjoyed talking. He knew people listen to you when you have money. He called his manager, Suraj Deshpande, to his room to discuss some new business idea. But Suraj knew his boss wanted to talk. He was ready for a new Congo story.

'Yes, *Patron*?' He sat across from his boss.

'Suraj, you know my net worth today is more than anyone else's in DRC. Most of the older generation of Indians and Pakistanis started their business at the same time, or they knew each other from East Africa; and most of them were somehow related. Clever, these people are. I tell you, marry among the same business community and the ties of the community only grows stronger. Incestuous to the core, all of them in their own Hindu, Muslim or Ismaili communities they are related. The young generation did not endure the struggles or hardships of theirs parents or grandparents. They were born in the lap of luxury. Their parents had already settled down in their own businesses, and made some smart investments. The young generation is well connected, they go back many, many years and know nothing but luxury, or they pretended to. Who knows now with changing times? Some of them are only prisoners of their past. The hard working fathers are struggling to hold on to the business, while the foreign educated sons dont't really understand the deeply complex West African market. Some are forced to return from USA and Canada to Congo and take charge of the family business; and they cannot handle the changed lifestyle or the business dynamics, and resort to easily available cheap marijuana. While some prodigal sons and daughters have taken their parents business to greater heights. They modified their business, branched out of their comfort zone, started new ventures and made more money.'

Manikchand continued his long story.

'The city is full of all types, of young and old Asian businessmen. They speak with that posh foreign accent. One thing is common. All of them have an adrenalin rushing, spine-chilling story to tell of 'the *peage*', or 'the pillage'. Most of them were young at that time and experienced it first-hand. When the economy was shaky and nationalism was at its peak. The government had taken over all the businesses run by foreigners and allotted them to local citizens or '*citoyens*'. Some actually invited their staff to take what they wanted from their shops and their houses. The Indian, Pakistanis, Greeks and Lebanese were badly hit. Their own staff or just any local could walk into their shop and claim it as their own. They were forced to leave their sprawling houses, shops, cars and pets; and escape to USA, Canada or Belgium. Some moved to Uganda, Kenya and Tanzania, but the situation was tough everywhere in Africa. Most of them managed to come back and restart, only to experience '*peage*' the second time, in 1997. They left the country again only to come back to reclaim and restart. Each one has his or her own tale of horror to tell, every family has that moment where they go quiet while discussing the coup *d'état*.'

Suraj Deshpande's phone rang, he looked at his boss for permission to leave the room.

'Go... Go. Do your work,' Manikchand dismissed him.

Manikchand regretted not experiencing pillage like the rich people. A poor man's struggle to survive never makes a good salon conversation.

'All these young Asian business men narrate their own horrific pillage and escape experiences to the expat women who ooh, aah, tsk tsk and hang on to every word of the story. No one is interested in a poor man's basic struggle to survive and feed his family while the country was burning. Poor people never make a good story. These men are real businessmen. They know how to market themselves using dramatic stories to grab attention of beautiful women. These men are too clever and too greedy. They want everything for themselves.' He hated their arrogance and attitude.

Champagne on the House

The music was loud and he didn't understand a word of the song that was playing. Manikchand was moving his body between two girls – slithering, writhing and dancing. He was at the very posh 'Club VIP'; the nightclub patronized by expats, rich locals and ladies of the night. Club VIP played the best music in town, and its dance floor could be viewed from every corner of the club. From the corner of his eye, he could see the super-rich Ashraf, surrounded by his hangers on and a bevy of international beauties. Ashraf, spent his childhood in Lubumbashi and later moved to the USA during the *peage*. He came back to head a chain of super markets in Congo, and various mines that his family owned. He always charmed and enthralled his audience by telling them, how they lived like royalty till reality of 'the *peage*' hit them. He always took the time to narrate his escape story.

'We had to rush out of Lubumbashi with my mother, sisters and cousins, and find an escape route. My father stayed back, hoping that things will improve and he would call us back soon. We left Lubumbashi with three hundred dollars stuck in my mother's *salwar* waistband and our plastic flip-flops' He would pause here and let the story have its impact. He always looked a bit distant at this point in his narration. He picked up his glass from the side table, sipped his Laphroaig and resumed the anecdote.

'My mother had the presence of mind. She cleverly and quickly ripped open some of my sister's stuffed toys, and hid her jewellery and some dollars, and stitched them back up. We carried all my sister's toys with us, knowing fully well that our lives depended on them. We went without food or drinks on our way to Kinshasa from Lubumbashi. A friend of my father managed to get us to the airport. We sat on the tarmac with other expats, too tired to talk. Finally, a Belgian peacekeeper – a close friend of my father, helped us board the flight out. I don't want to talk about death or destruction that we saw on our way. I want to wipe away those horrible memories…' Ashraf was a gentleman to the core. He would always stop at this point in his story, and ask his guests if they wanted another round of drinks. He made sure that all glasses were refilled including his.

'Coming back to my story. Suddenly we had become refugees. Nowhere to go. Language was a huge issue, we spoke Lingala, Gujrati and French. We landed in USA with $300 in hand. Initially, we lived with some distant relatives, and later moved into a small apartment. My father, peace be upon him, somehow managed to send us money every month. That's how we knew he was alive. Those were bad days. My mother was used to living like a queen. She had ten domestic helps including cooks, drivers, cleaners and gardeners working in the Lubumbashi house. Now she did everything on her own. She turned old overnight. She was cooking, cleaning and looking after us. But she managed to keep our spirits up. "Daddy will make things fine and soon and we will be back in Congo. If you have enjoyed the sweet ripe *paw-paws* of Congo, it always call you back," she would reassure us, and try and make us laugh. I was sad to see my mother's soft hand turn rough. Her trademark, once poker-straight bob, was now frizzy and limp shoulder length hair. She would ask us to pray for peace and safety of our father. I got around fine, with my university, though I missed my Lubumbashi house, garden and swimming pool. My sister was badly affected. She suddenly started stammering. She would wake up in the middle of the night sweating and screaming, "*Mamman, coupe d'états*", or "*Mamman ou est pappy?*" Every loud sound reminded her of the gunshots back home. She had to undergo therapy to recover from her sense of loss and trauma.'

The women were always enchanted by Ashraf's stories. Tonight was no different. Ashraf sat among the eager eyed expat women, entertaining them with stories about life in Africa.

Manikchand swore under his breath. 'Motherfucker has a beautiful wife and now he is pushing his luck with all these women. Some men are born lucky. Here I have to struggle for everything.' He walked up to Ashraf's table and shook hands with him. What a firm handshake. Manikchand admired Ashraf's muscles, rippling under his short sleeved, deep V-neck t-shirt.

'Ashraf *bhai*, you look like Salman Khan. *Ek dum mas*t body *shody*!' Manikchand said, as he sat on the empty chair next to Ashraf.

He touched Ashraf's biceps and said, '*Bhai*, you are getting younger by the day. Six pack stomach and strong biceps – share the secret with me also.' Ashraf smiled, revealing those deep dimples that everyone loved, and blew out perfect circles of smoke from the cigar he was smoking.

Manikchand snapped his fingers at the waiter passing by. '*Papa yaka, Pesa* champagne.' He personally poured champagne for Ashraf and everybody that sat around him. 'It's on me guys… *Sante*!' Manikchand toasted His eyes scanned the psychedelic nightclub, as he tried to ascertain whether people had noticed that he was sitting at the same table as Ashraf; and that he was the one ordering for champagne. He knew people were watching.

'Inviting envy is good. It means I am a *Vrais patron*! A true boss!' He smiled and his hands automatically reached up to his amulet and he stroked it. '*Dieu Merci*! Old Juju is very powerful indeed,' he thought.

Ashraf continued with his story to entertain his coterie. He was telling them about the history behind the huge presence of Indians and Pakistanis in Congo. Manikchand listened like an ardent student, memorizing every word.

'I can use these stories later to impress other women,' he thought. Ashraf was entertaining a big group of new expats in Kinshasa. They were mostly from different embassies and some high officials from the United Nations. Ashraf sipped his champagne and signalled the waiter to change the glass. It wasn't chilled enough. He put his cigar on the ashtray and started his practiced monologue...

'Many adventurous Indians and Pakistanis, took a risk and started their own small businesses around the 1940s, 50s and 60s in Congo. With their hard work and determination, their businesses spread across to Bunia, Goma and Lubumbashi. Small shops belonging to Indians sprang up in small towns. Nothing fancy, but they were quick to identify the needs of the locals. The shop was often a shack or a room filled with things for sale. The locals flocked to buy what was so far a luxury for them. Traders would come on boats, to stock up for villages further in the bush. Indians and Pakistanis were smart businessmen. They partnered with some local businesswomen who bought goods on credits and sold them on *piroques,* or little boats to villagers who lived in swampy areas. A few of their business partners were warlords, while some were powerful people in the local militia. Later they did not physically harm them, during the first and the second *peage*.'

'The shop was usually a small cement-floored room or a garage in a building, and everything displayed on the floor was for sale. The items, so far considered luxury and enjoyed only by the city dwellers, were now available in the small towns and villages. The most precious were the enamel plates, utensils and basins. Eating '*fufu* with *pondu*' was never this easy –, the plates could hold a small mountain of *fufu* and soup without everything leaking. The plastic sheets sold in these shops were used to dry the cassava, on. Small kerosene cooking stoves and lamps were huge hits. All items were arranged on the shop floor, along with notebooks, refill pens, candles, match box and bright fabric. Indians and Pakistanis dared to establish and run businesses where the Europeans wouldn't venture.' He continued.

'They were the new entrepreneurs. Soon they invited their poor country cousins from Gujarat, Sindh and some parts of Pakistan to Congo, to join their growing business. They also had friends and family who were struggling in Tanzania, Kenya, Uganda and Bujumbura join them or send their sons to work with them. These people were already familiar with Africa, though the Francophone Africa was very different.' Ashraf signalled for a refill. The women were visibly impressed.

'And then?' asked a young American diplomat.

Ashraf took a deep breath and continued, 'There is something about the trading community from the North West of India. The Sindhis and Gujaratis, with no fancy degrees from big business schools were running successful businesses using, a unique model evolved by them. Nobody could replicate their business model. They gradually spread from East Africa to West Africa, and realized that in order to survive and prosper, they had to maintain a symbiotic relationship. Marriage was one way to strengthen their ties. They were quick to learn Lingala, the local language of the Congo, and adapt to the local traditions. Their capacity to adapt and work hard is unparalleled. Most Indians in East

Africa spoke fluent Swahili and when they moved to Congo, they spoke *Lingala* like a native. The women often worked alongside the men – though they were very discreet, initially. They were super innovative in the kitchen. These women kept their traditional cuisine and customs alive. The wives whipped up *'dahi vadas'* and *'Gulab jamuns'* with local bread. *'Shaak'* and *'Daal'* were customized with local lentils and vegetables. The wives often competed, to create typical Indian dishes with locally sourced ingredients. My grandma was obviously the best!' Ashraf paused again.

'*Cherie, yaka,*' he called the waitress. 'Change my glass.'

'Ashraf, tell us more. It is so fascinating,' said a Swiss doctor.

'Soon, Indians started to be innovative with their business ideas. Some started small grocery shops that exclusively sold Indian products, along with video and audio cassettes. While few started showing Indian movies on television and the VCR player at night to the local population. This increased the sale of drinks, snacks and bread at night. The small grocery stores eventually expanded, and either became a chain of grocery stores; big super markets; or restaurant-bars. Business expanded, there were more relatives off the boat, willing to work hard to make money. The relatives toiled, sweated and endured to increase profits, save money with a hope of starting out on their own. They were itching to branch out on their own, the terrain was tough but familiar, and now they knew the tricks. Soon with all the money acquired, invested and resources multiplied, the *patrons* were travelling and expanding their empire.'

'The next generation got lucky, they had a battery of staff running and maintaining the show – mostly their relatives or distant cousins. The business model also changed with time. When an employee broke away to venture out on his own, and the owner was sure of his business acumen, he would also invest cash in his former employees business, and share the profits. The *patron* didn't really get down to dirty business, but still earned profit.

Investing became a business in itself. Few Indians started lending money for interest to start new business ventures. Others would deliver money to Angola, Rwanda, Burundi, Uganda, Kenya, Tanzania and to Gujarat, to family members and business partners. They made quick and big profits, and invested in real estate in Belgium, London and Kinshasa. They also invested in mines. In the meantime, the original *Patrons* were still very involved with their work, while their children were free to attend universities in America or Europe; and were free to do what they wanted to jet ski on the Congo River, hunt or chase women,' Ashraf said, and he laughed.

Then he continued, 'According to some people we lead a fancy life hobnobbing only with the super elite clique. *N'est pas*, Manikchand?' he said, as he slapped Manikchand on the back and laughed. 'But guys, I still work very hard and am very involved in my business. My only luxury is golf, which I play every day at 5 p.m.; and my workout with my personal trainer from 8 a.m. to 10 a.m.'

There were loud murmurs in the audience.

A young British diplomat who was mostly quiet throughout the narration said, 'Wow! Your story sounds like "*Out of Africa*".

A blonde woman piped in, 'Ashraf, you should write a book about your experiences. You have lived such a unique life. I was talking to Bilal, Rajiv and Sahil, your childhood friends from Lubumbashi. They had a similar fascinating story to tell.' The manager discreetly added five more chairs for Ashraf's close childhood friends, who joined in. His cousin Anita who was married to a Belgian diplomat, was visiting Ashraf in Kinshasa for the first time after getting married. Many more old friends dropped in at Club VIP in to relive old times. They were laughing and talking about their childhood. Their spouses hung on to every word they uttered.

'Such fairy tale lives you guys lived,' sighed the blonde. 'You must write that book, Ashraf,' she said.

'Oh! Ashraf's life wasn't like a fairy tale at all. In fact, it was more like Mowgli's. Should I tell them about your escapades Ashraf?' asked Yusuf, with a smile. 'Remember the time you jumped off the old rope bridge at Black River, and stayed underwater till your mother cried and your father threatened to beat you up?' Yusuf was laughing.

'Oh, remember the time when Ashraf told his old cook that their new television was white man's juju, or voodoo and the old cook wouldn't enter the room?' Anita, his cousin chipped in.

'I remember how when we went camping to Zongo Falls, Ashraf would throw pebbles at the women who would go to pee behind the bushes. He told everyone that the bushes were haunted,' another person chipped in. There were more stories, more laughs and more drinks. Ashraf ordered another bottle of Glen and made a toast to the spirit of *Kin la Belle*, which is what they called their beautiful city.

'There is no place on Earth quite like Kinshasa. Raise your glasses,' shouted Ashraf.

'*Sante*!' Everyone screamed together.

'Kin is sick man. I love the night life here,' said 20 years old Raghav, who had just returned to the city after finishing his education in Miami. 'Uncle Ashraf, thanks for the drinks,' Raghav shouted over the music.

'Dude, we are buddies now. Don't uncle me. *Bienvenue a Kin la belle*. Welcome to the big boys club. Now you can come play poker and tennis with us. Did I tell you that while growing up I had a huge crush on your mom?' Ashraf said, and everyone laughed. Manikchand sat amongst them. He, desperately wanted to be accepted by the suave, sophisticated and educated children who belonged to the original Indian migrant families. They were extremely different from the other Indians he knew. As far as he was concerned, they weren't even 'true Indians'; even though they spoke Gujarati with a strange accent, and peppered their conversations with the phrase '*bloody chodu*'. This educated set of second and third generation Indians came from typical old money, and had too much class. They had deep roots in Africa and very deep pockets. Manikchand knew that the only similarity between them, and him, was the glass of single malt they held in their hands.

Manikchand always said, 'Looking rich is important and even smelling good is very important.' His thoughts were changing with time.

'Somehow, your body just knows what scent to give off. It emits a bad odour, an overwhelming stench when you are poor. Try getting close to a poor person when he talks, and you'll find that his mouth smells just like one of the open gutters near his house. Same to same, no difference. A man is the reflection of the gutter he keeps! And, when you become rich you smell good, just like the light blue ocean they show on a TV commercial. When you have money and you are rich, you automatically smell good,' declared the new millionaire to his hangers on. He was obsessed with his nose. He loved to spray on intense, expensive perfumes. The expensive smell made him realize that he had finally become rich. He noticed how rich people always smelt fresh, without even trying too hard. He observed how the rich looked like they had just stepped out of a shower, and he wanted to figure out how their hair was always wet, jet black and permanently flicked in place. He liked to closely observe their nails, and noticed that they were always clipped, clear and clean. He saw that their hands were are always smooth and shiny, just like the Vaseline advertisement during winters. His own hands were dry and covered in scars, while his nails were yellow, rough and brittle.

Now, he made sure that he always carried a hand sanitizer, lotion and wet wipes in his car. 'I have to shake too many hands. Too many infections can be transferred just through touch. Can't take any risks,' he instructed his driver. The ice box in the trunk had a few bottles of Moet and Chandon, a few foldable chairs and six glasses. He was a keen observer and now tried to live like them – the rich people that surrounded him. He was quick to offer a bottle to celebrate, and these days there were enough reasons to pop the bubbly. He felt it coming – the social acceptability in the close knit and super elite society of Kinshasa. "They will accept me into their circle soon." He hoped.

His hand touched the little amulet around his neck, "Make them accept me, keep them coming," he said in his mind. He always communicated with his amulet. "The amulet is my personal mobile phone. It conveys my thoughts to the universe. Stay there, *pappa* and continue to work your magic for me." he said to the amulet.

Manikchand had heard about a book called 'The Secret', from one of the many girls he had spent a night with in Matadi, the port city. He enjoyed his time with the local girls, while waiting for the containers. One such girl told him about the book. Before leaving she had gifted him a CD of the book. Manikchand rarely received gifts. 'A rare act,' he thought.

Cherie, c'est pour toi,' she had said, before keeping it on the table beside him. She counted her money and left.

He thought it was a music album and decided to play it on his long drive back from Matadi to Kinshasa. But when he heard the CD it changed his thoughts and his life. 'Oh, motherfucker! This is very simple. You get what you ask for. You have to send signals to the Universe! *Chalo*, I will do that.' He always wanted to thank that girl for the CD, and wanted to send her some money but he just couldn't remember her name or the names of any of her friends. 'Aaah the problem of picking too many girls. They come and go. If they are good, you use them again, otherwise fuck them and forget them. Simple. No *lafda* and no court case. They can take you to court any day to say that you are the father of the child they are expecting,' Manikchand thought to himself. He had seen so many of his friends being summoned by the court. They were forced to pay a living allowance because some girl had accused them of being the father of the child they were carrying. 'No no no... night over and relationship over, with the nightclub pick up type girls. I am too smart! Too smart *pappa*!' he laughed. He never failed to send signals to the universe. He wanted to be rich. Rich like the old monied people. He wanted to be a *Patron*. *Patron* like the real one. He wanted women, mistresses of all colours, fame and most of all ultimate power.

Ramesh... Matatu, Matata and Mobulu

He had suffered twenty years of excruciating humiliation. Twenty years of doing petty odd jobs for various, distant, arrogant cousins; and friends of friends. They never failed to rub in the fact that they were doing him a huge favour by employing him, and that he was a part of their monthly charity.

'*Ar ra ra. Saala*, they act as if they are Mother Teresa. I hate that patronizing tone. I bring in money for your businesses, so don't give me "*ehsan*" bullshit,' he muttered to himself. 'I hate you all and one day I will come back to get your expensive ass'. No matter who hired him, they always made it a point to tell him that they had hired him despite having no vacancies, because they felt sorry for his family. "The bastards never utter a polite acknowledgement, regarding all the income I generate for them. I have spent the last twenty years waking up at the crack of dawn, and then commuting to work via public transport. Every morning I squeeze into smelly rusty *matatus*, packed with local men, women, children, animals and birds. Throughout the journey, the stench of bad breath, sweat and fish, permeates the air." He sighed.

Ramesh woke up early so that he would be on time to catch the first *matatu*. He did not want to be late for work. The sun was hidden behind the *Harmattan* sky. His asthma became worse when the winds from the north carried red dust over to the city, and covered the entire landscape with a rusty hue. The city looked desolate, dreary and dry. The trees looked eerie with their dusty red leaves, which drooped at the edges, as if they were desperately seeking water from the dry, cracked earth. They could have easily been mistaken for props from a Nigerian horror movie. He was wheezing. The kids were falling sick, the God forsaken wind only brought in sickness and more work. All the houses and shops in the city had to be constantly dusted, since the red stubborn film of dust would keep returning "I hate how my nose always feels stuffy. I feel tiny dry granules of sand stuffed in my nostrils. One sneeze, *'aanchoo'* and out came a gooey red liquid mixed with sand. The air is so full of sand, I can chew it." Ramesh hated the Harmattan season.

'Arre, you open your mouth to talk and in goes the sand. The hot dusty *'loo'* in India is much better. This season is worse than African summer. Anyway making comparisons is futile. Africa never lets you relax. Life is a constant struggle for the poor. The oppressive fiery sun burns and beats you down, and then it soothes you with the violent rains. What a great sense of humour the gods have? Once the rain comes, the roofs leak, the stored food gets spoiled and all kinds of disease break out. And then the dusty *harmattan* arrives,' Ramesh said. He grabbed his wife from behind, while she was preparing a cup of *masala chai* for him.

'Besharam. Let me finish my work. Go to work now. There is nothing in the house. Bring a sack of rice, and some milk and sugar, on your way back.' She said.

'Chain se humko khabhi aapney jeeney na diya,' he hummed, while spitting up phlegm and red dust. He took a few sips of the *chai* and then dunked two pieces of rusk biscuits and slurped it.

'Kem, no sugar? Saali, mari wife has become too *matata.'* He yelled at his wife, 'Next time add more sugar to my *chai*", and rushed out. 'It is important to be rich. That way one gets to travel in an AC car, eat *bhajiya*, and drink Rum and Coke while it rains. No tension, boss!' he thought while

climbing into the *matatu*. He was busy imagining himself sitting in an, air-conditioned SUV, while being driven around by a driver. Lost in his daydream, he absentmindedly stepped on something that felt squishy. When he looked down he saw a small baby crocodile staring right back at him.

'*Bachao! Bachao!*' he yelled, before realizing that no one could understand him. '*Aides moi,*' he screamed, as he jumped on to a seat. That's when he spotted more baby crocodiles. They were all coming out of a plastic bag on the floor. The other passengers started screaming and abusing the crocodile seller while the *matatu* driver ignored the commotion, and continued to drive like a manic. The crocodile seller had promised to give the driver two per cent share of the profits. The passengers continued to scream while the baby crocodiles looked petrified.

'It's all about having a smart business idea boss,' Ramesh thought to himself, as he looked at the sack. He wanted to explore the crocodile business in detail now, knowing that it could help him earn a little extra money on the side. The crocodile seller, with his sack full of baby crocodiles got off just before Gombe – the expat residential area. Ramesh decided to follow the seller and got off the bus as well. In the meantime, the other passengers stuck their heads out of the bus window, to continue yelling abuses at the seller.

'*Eh, toi, Mon frère. Kanga* sack. Crocodiles are too dangerous. You sell crocodile for meat to *Mundele*?' Ramesh asked, as he caught up with the seller.

'No, no. *Lasse moi tranquil. Eh! Toi? Arret le question,*' the crocodile seller said, wanting to get rid of Ramesh. He started to run. But, Ramesh was quick to catch him by his wrist. He then proceeded to grill him, until he had found out everything he wanted to.

The seller had figured out that pet crocodiles were the

most 'in' thing among the rich locals, as well as some of the expat communities. It attracted women to their parties, and the conversations revolved around the exotic pets of the owner. He told Ramesh that the big weekend houses in *Mon Fleury* and *Ma Campagne* had mini zoos. He described the villas, which he said had huge ornamental gardens, ornate gazebos and big pools; as well as exotic pets like deer, crocodiles, monkeys and parakeets. Ramesh made a mental note to suggest to his *Patron* to add a few crocodiles to his sprawling house.

His present boss, Lakha *bhai*, was a second generation Gujarati Indian in Congo. "Lakha *bhai* refuses to acknowledge that he is Indian. He has a Belgian passport and is very European in his ways. The only Indian thing about him is that he smokes *beedis* in private, which his staff brings back from India for him. Lakha *bhai*? The less said of him, the better," Ramesh thought.

Lakha *bhai's* father, Ramji *bhai* had started off by selling batteries and refill pens in Kisangani. He later moved to Lubumbashi, and struck gold by starting a small supermarket, He then branched off into mining and timber business. Ramji *bhai* understood the art of making money. Ramji *bhai* lost his wife while she was giving birth to their son. He never re-married or chased other women; he was too busy building an empire for his son to inherit. He also wanted to forget his pain, for he truly loved his wife. She died in front of him because of excessive bleeding. He couldn't do anything to save her life. He had a new born baby to take care of. His young cleaner Mamma Patty, took charge of little Lakshman from the moment he was born. She called him *mobulu* (naughty), and *mobulu* he was. She never married or had her own children for 'Baby Lucky' was her life. Ramji *bhai* appreciated everything Mamma did for his son, and bought her a plot of land to show his gratitude.

Ramji *bhai* had completely immersed himself in his business. But he missed home and family. He invited his brother, who was at that time working in Bujumbura with a Greek businessman. Ramji *bhai* offered him a good job in his business. He wanted his son, Lakshman *aka* baby Lucky *aka* Lakha *bhai* to have a close contact with family. He wanted his son to have someone of his 'own' around him.

Ramji *bhai*'s brother, Jyoti *bhai* was nothing like him. He liked to chase women and drink good wine. After moving to Lubumbashi, as per his brother's request he eventually married a local politician's daughter, and started his own transport business. His children, the half caste or *metisse* as they were called there became baby Lucky's family. Lakshman or Lakha as he came to be known, grew up in Lubumbashi among the Belgians and his *metisse* cousins; and soaked in their way of life. The children were educated at the Belgian school, and later Lakha and his cousins moved to Brussels, to pursue higher studies.

Lakha *bhai* was fair skinned, *gora chitta* like a European. He spoke French like the Belgians, and enjoyed indulging in *moules-frites* and French wine. He was very particular about his coffee, it had to be black and served at a particular temperature. Many of his servants, had had the experience of having a piping hot shot of espresso thrown at them. Only Papa Mofi, their old family retainer knew how to serve him the right *petite dejeneur*. Croissants, cheese and coffee. Followed by two fresh *beedis* from India. People would often remark that while Lakha *bhai's* complexion was light his heart and ways of life were dark. He had a mean streak in him, which was a sharp contrast from his father.

Ramji *bhai* helped everyone in his community, regardless

of whether they were Indians, locals or Pakistanis; although he was partial to the Hindu community. He had helped many Hindus in Congo with setting up their own small business, by lending them money. His only condition was that they had to make a profit. As long as they did that, he would remain their business partner. This model worked perfectly for him, and he owned shares in many businesses. Ramji *bhai* used his money to generate more money. He contributed to the construction of a local women's hospital – in memory of his wife – as well as a community centre for the Hindus. He helped the *Hare Krishna Community* set up a temple, and many locals were encouraged to join the group. The devotees would often perform *bhajans* in his house. He also donated money to various orphanages and women's shelters, around the city. He was a generous donor and was highly respected in the community. Ramji *bhai* was a popular philanthropist, and was always invited as the chief guest to the different charity events organized by the International Women's Club and the Asian Women's Club.

Lakha *bhai,* after finishing his studies, returned from Brussels to help his father run their family business. However, instead of helping his father, Lakha spent most of his time fighting with him over business ethics. The employees would often hear them argue outside of their closed wood panelled, air-conditioned office.

Today, when Ramesh reached the office in *Marche Centrale,* he could hear his boss's angry voice. Lakha *bhai* was yelling and shouting. He wanted to break away from the business and take his share with him.

'Pa, if you don't like my style of doing business, then let's part ways,' he said in a harsh tone.

'You are still inexperienced and too brash, Lakshman. Learn the ropes before you take off on your own,' Ramji *bhai* responded, calmly. He paused and then continued, 'Learn to treat our employees well. Most of them are our relatives, or relatives of our friends. They are not your servants. You need to change your attitude if you want to be successful in your business ventures.'

'Oh, fuck off, pa,' Lakha *bhai*, retorted. Ramji *bhai* was taken aback, he had never been insulted like this; moreover, he knew his staff was listening to their conversation.

From that day on, Ramji *bhai* started to spend less time at the office, and more on the construction site of the '*Ramji – Lakshmanji Charitable Hospital,*' that he was building on the outskirts of the city.

Lakha *bhai* continued with his aggressive ways, and to exploit people. He reduced his employees' salaries and cut all their benefits, which included the payment of school fees and reimbursement for medical expenses. 'Go and find another job,' would be his curt response whenever someone complained or protested. Lakha *bhai* expanded his father's mining business; and was the first person in the country, who was able to get a Chinese business partner. This allowed him to bring in advanced digging machines from China. He also opened a Chinese Restaurant and a supermarket, in partnership with the biggest Chinese company in Kinshasa. Lakha *bhai* changed the rules of the game. There was no time for compassion, family or friends. He did not believe in offering charity or giving out loans. He was driven by only one passion, and that was money.

Ramji *bhai* thought marriage would change his son for the better, and so he started looking for a girl for him.

Ramji *bhai* first met Meena in Delhi, with her father. She was young, fresh and full of life. He soon arranged for her to meet his son. He sincerely hoped that she would bring out the humane side in his son. Lakha *bhai*, thankfully agreed to the marriage alliance arranged by his father. The reason he agreed so easily was that he knew Meena was an only child, and he would inherit all of her father's wealth. Lakha *bhai* was a smart businessman, and always loved a good profitable deal.

'Get ready to party, for that is what life will be like for you in Kinshasa – one big party! I will give you the keys to my apartment in Brussels, and my house in Toronto. You can take a flight to Delhi whenever you want. You will live like a queen,' Lakha *bhai* told her, when he met her for the first time at the Taj Hotel, in Delhi. Meena instantly fell for Lakha *bhai's* good looks and charm. They decided to hold their wedding ceremony at the same hotel. Friends and family were flown in from Africa, Canada and Hong Kong. It was a fairy tale wedding. Meena, daughter of a rich Delhi businessman, was marrying the only son of a business tycoon from Africa.

Ramji *bhai* flew in some important ministers, the head of the Army and a few famous lawyers from Congo. He was happy for his son and daughter-in-law. His only regret was that his wife was not alive to celebrate the beautiful marriage of their only son.

After spending a whole month in Europe on a magical honeymoon, the couple headed back to Kinshasa. Ramji *bhai* gifted them his own five-bedroom penthouse, which overlooked the Congo River. He moved into a more modern, but compact apartment, on the boulevard recently constructed by his Lebanese business partner. Ramji *bhai* now wanted to get into construction. He could predict a future for these low-rise apartment buildings, with a swimming pool and a gym. All the short-term United Nations crowd, embassies and multinational companies, were looking for compact and modern accommodation. He was already in the middle of negotiating a deal that would give him ownership of some old decrepit Belgian houses, in the city centre.

The newly-wed couple soon settled into their new home. Mamma Patty, Lakha *bhai's* nanny lived with them. She instantly fell in love with Meena. Meena spent her first month in Kinshasa, learning how to bake the perfect meringue and cook the most perfect *biryani*, from the family cook. Though there was no need for her to go into the kitchen, since the staff worked like clockwork. However, she found solace in putting together a gourmet meal. Her father-in-law relished her cooking. She would often invite him over for a meal. If he could not come, she would have her driver deliver food to him. She also made an effort to learn French, to communicate with her staff and the locals in Kinshasa. She loved her new house, and every evening she would sit in the balcony and drink the tea, while admiring the vast expanse of the Congo River. She had read somewhere that it was the deepest river in the world.

Meena's life soon took a drastic turn. It became turbulent and unpredictable, as Lakha *bhai's* real personality began to reveal itself. She hated that he flirted with all kinds of women, stayed out late into the night and took frequent business trips.

'I am a Casanova. The quintessential, good-looking, rich brat. Don't expect me to be stuck to you all the time,' he had said to her one night. Lakha *bhai* liked to party a lot. He enjoyed the company of girls and would often entertain his old flames. He was happiest around his *metisse* cousins, who lived off their father's money. Lakha *bhai* also adored his uncle Jyoti and his Congolese aunt, as they always indulged him like he was still a child. His uncle continued sleeping around with local women, and fathering *metisse* children. He and his cousins often joked about the fertility of the old man. Many *metisse* boys and girls would turn up at their house claiming to be his son, or daughter. The family managed to turn this into a joke. 'Anyone with light skin in DRC is a potential brother or sister!' Ramji *bhai* was the only one who did not laugh at such jokes.

Lakha *bhai* eventually took complete control of his father's business. He was driven by his desire to be the richest businessman in Congo. He had many ideas and he wanted to implement them. Ramesh was a good resource. He understood Lakha *bhai's* hunger for new business. They worked well as a team. Ramesh was busy, like never before. Meanwhile, the corruption in the country reached its peak, the currency fell and the general economy was at an all-time low. Their company had to constantly deal with the hardships that came with such circumstances, but Ramesh and Lakha *bhai* managed to make their business profitable. Both had the same thought process and worked hard. Lakha *bhai* recognized Ramesh's special talent as a wheeler – dealer, but always treated him as a regular employee and was usually brusque with him. Ramesh loved to crack bawdy jokes and laugh, but Lakha *bhai* never smiled. He was unusually stoic around his subordinates. Meena on the other hand treated Ramesh like her brother.

While no one cared about Ramesh as a person; whenever Meena saw him she would greet him by saying, '*Jai Shri Krishna*, Ramesh *bhai. Kem cho*?'

This would make Lakha *bhai* angry. 'We don't socialize with our servants,' he would tell her. So she started to ignore Ramesh when her husband was around, but would treat him with sisterly affection when she was alone.

Ramesh remembered how a few days after Meena – or Meena *bhabi,* as he called her – had arrived in Kinshasa, he had taken her to the *Marche Centrale*. Lakha *bhai's* new bride was curious to see the heart of Kinshasa, and Ramesh had volunteered to take her around. Lakha *bhai* obviously had no knowledge of this *tour de ville,* or he would have instantly forbidden it.

'I feel like Alice in Wonderland, Ramesh *bhai,*' Meena *bhabhi* said. He looked at her amused, she was like a child in a candy store.

'Who is Alice? Your friend?' Ramesh asked Meena *bhabhi.* She responded by laughing hysterically.

'Wow! What beautiful drapes adorn the shops of Fabric Lane, on *Avenue de Commerce.* Look, they stock everything from the most gorgeous chiffons, to chamois satin and linen. Ramesh *bhai*, this reminds me of Lajpat Nagar Market in New Delhi,' she said, happily. She decided to buy a pristine white peek-a-boo fabric to make a summer dress.

'Are you from Congo?' she asked the shopkeeper.

'Me? No. I am from Lebanon. I have been working in this shop for over a year now. I miss my small village in the south of Lebanon. But I have many friends from my village here. My uncle owns this shop. I live in a shared apartment with other Lebanese boys who work for my uncle,' the shopkeeper replied, and handed her a packet. He was very excited and chatty. Meena was amused.

'The nightclubs here are very good. Do you dance?' he asked Meena, in his Arabic accented English. 'I'm also engaged to a girl from my village who is beautiful like you, I am going to go back to my village next month, for the wedding. Then I shall return with her,' he said, before taking out a picture of his fiancé from his wallet and showing it to her.

'Beautiful indeed!' said Meena *bhabhi.* 'Good luck with your marriage.' She paid him and walked out.

'*Inshallah,* next year I will have my own shop,' he confided. 'You must come; I make good price for you'. Ramesh was amused and impressed by his ambition. '*Yalla* bye,' said Meena *bhabhi*. She rushed out admiring her purchase.

As soon as they left the store Meena exclaimed, 'Ramesh *bhai*! Look there!' She pointed at a Congolese lady dressed in a bright maroon sari replete with jingling bangles, chandelier earrings and *mang teeka*. The lady was crossing the street. Meena *bhabhi* made a dash for her, completely ignoring the chaotic traffic.

'*Sil vous plait*,' she yelled, while gasping for breath. The lady gave Meena a quizzical look.

'*Vous éte trés belle*,' Meena *bhabhi* said. She burst into peals of giggles.

'*Merci, merci, merci*,' the Congolese lady said, as she clapped with glee. She then looked at Meena *bhabhi* very seriously and said, 'If you think I am that beautiful, why you no find Indian groom for me? I hear that Indian men are very family oriented and don't usually divorce. Look at Shah Rukh Khan, he has just one wife for all these years!'

'I promise you *ma soeur*. I will find you a *tres beau* Indian *Mari*.' Ramesh joined in. 'Tell me, how did you drape the sari and where did you get it from?' Meena asked. The Congolese lady informed her that there was an Indian shop just 50 meters away; and the Indian lady who was running it, pre-stitched the saris according to individual size, so that they could be slipped on like a skirt.

'You want to see?' she asked Meena *bhabhi*.

'Of course! Let's go!' Meena *bhabhi* replied, excitedly. They held hands and started walking like old friends.

'No, Meena *bhabhi,* you can't walk around here with strangers like this,' objected Ramesh. 'Lakha *bhai* will get angry if he hears of this. Let's go back.' Ramesh requested.

'*Ca va c'est pas grave,*' the Congolese lady said. They high-fived each other, and then continued to walk.

'Oh my God! Look, Ramesh *bhai*, they sell everything. Saris, *salwar kameez*, *jootis*, fake jewellery, hairpins, and ribbons. It's bling, bling, bling all the way,' Meena *bhabhi* laughed. The shop was choc-a-block with local and Indian ladies. 'Oohs' and 'aahs' could be heard, as the clients picked up stuff to buy. Meena *bhabhi* looked dazed as she stood and looked around.

'*Bhabhi*, eyebrow first floor *par hota hai,*' said a young Indian boy, who was sitting at the counter. The poor boy was being teased and bullied by all the young girls in the shop.

'*Ohh, acha,*' Meena said, and then proceeded to make her way up the stairs with her new friend. Ramesh followed her.

'*Bhabhi*, please lets go back home. Lakha *bhai* will kill me for bringing you here.' he pleaded.

The first floor was a mad house beauty parlour. The Congolese lady introduced Meena *bhabhi* to the Indian lady who ran the parlour. She narrated her entire life history to Meena *Bhabhi* in one breath.

'*Bhabhi*, there is a huge market for Indian cosmetics, clothes and beauty treatments among the local population. I started off by doing facials and eyebrows from my house. I came from a small city in Gujarat and was married to my husband at the age of 20. When I arrived in Kinshasa as a young bride, I was completely bored. My husband was busy at work, and I didn't speak any French. I started off by doing facials and threading for my Indian neighbours.'

Meena Bhabhi felt claustrophobic. In one corner of the beauty parlour, two local women stripped to try on their pre-stitched saris, while in another corner a facial was in progress. Amidst all the hustle bustle, someone could be heard crying out in pain, as the beautician threaded her eyebrows. One woman was screaming that she wanted her sari ensemble ready by the evening, as she had a party to attend. Meena *bhabhi* couldn't breathe. She hadn't seen anything like this before. She was overwhelmed by the smell of incense sticks, which were placed in the various framed posters of Aishwarya Rai, Sushmita Sen and Bipasha Basu.

'Let's go, *bhabhi*,' Ramesh said, noticing how uncomfortable she was. A few minutes later he escorted her out.

'Don't forget to find an Indian groom for me!' hollered the Congolese lady, as she bid them goodbye.

'Ramesh *bhai*, I am hungry. Let's get some bananas,' Meena *bhabhi* said. Ramesh took her around the corner. Meena *bhabhi* couldn't believe what she saw next, a local man was sitting there and doling out lunch packets to a group of Indian men. She decided to go to talk to him. The Congolese man informed her that he worked for an Indian lady, who cooked meals for Indian bachelors.

'Madame, I come here every day with *poori-aloo*, *dabeli* or *parathas* and sell it for this lady.' Meena *bhabhi* bought herself a *dabeli* (a spicy Indian burger) and ate it then and there, much to the amusement of all the Indian boys.

'Thank God, they don't know who she is, or else word about her behaviour will quickly spread,' thought Ramesh. He didn't want any problems with Lakha *bhai*, his boss.

'Madame, take my employer's phone number. She caters for parties as well,' the old man said.

'Meena *bhabhi*, enough. Let's go back,' Ramesh begged. He almost regretted bringing her to Central Market. A Chinese vendor suddenly appeared out of nowhere and said, 'Come visit my wife's massage parlour.'

Meena turned to Ramesh and said, 'Let's go check it out.' She was excited again.

'Meena *bhabhi*, that place is meant for entertainment of men. Let's go now.' He walked towards the car. She had no choice but to follow him. Ramesh dropped her home and took a taxi to work.

Lakha *bhai* encouraged Ramesh as a business resource in office, but outside the office he did not even bother to acknowledge him. Although he often paid Ramesh extra money, for any additional work he did. No one could handle the police and *Douane*, like Ramesh. Everyone agreed that he was a good resource, but very complicated. Whenever Ramesh visited Lakha *bhai's* home to drop off money or documents, he was never invited to enter. The old nanny would collect the package at the door and hand it to Lakha *bhai*. But if Meena *bhabhi* was alone, she would often invite him in for a cup of *masala chai* and small talk. 'You treat me like a, real brother Meena *bhabhi*,' Ramesh would often joke with her. He genuinely liked Meena *bhabhi*. She was very warm and welcoming to him.

Ramesh always felt small and insulted. He worked around the clock for Lakha *bhai*, but he never received any respect or enough money. His salary package included a measly 500 dollars, along with a small house outside the city limits. The house was actually the servant quarter of what used to be a warehouse that Lakha *bhai* had once rented out to an Ivorian businessman. It was Ramesh who negotiated that deal; otherwise the warehouse would have remained vacant and decrepit. He continued to work there because he didn't have too many options.

Ramesh kept a mental record of all the insults he endured in his life. He would get even. He knew that the day he would get the pleasure of revenge, was not too far away.

Soon, Meena *bhabi* was expecting her first child. She was experiencing severe morning sickness and it took a toll on her health. Lakha *bhai* decided to send her to Brussels. He did not have the time or patience to cater to his wife's tantrums, or to help look after her health. A few months after becoming pregnant, she moved to Brussels to deliver her baby. The child needed to have a Belgian passport like its father and grandfather. Lakha *bhai's* old nanny, Mamma Patty accompanied her, along with his old cook; as someone needed to be with her and look after her. Her father was busy with his business in Delhi, and she had no mother or mother-in-law to help her out. She was on her own, with only her domestic staff there as her support.

Lakha *bhai* was happy to have his own space. He relished his freedom and his empty house. He wanted to be left alone in his house, so that he could happily laze around in his silk bathrobe.

Meena often called Ramesh, to get updates on her husband. 'Ramesh *bhai*, I am very happy here in Brussels. It is so beautiful and peaceful. These are the happiest days of my life,' she told him. She called him once in the middle of the night, crying hysterically, 'Ramesh *bhai*, you know what? The old cook Papa Matondo has run away. He left the house early this morning, and is still not back as yet. Lucky will be so mad.'

Ramesh tried to console her, and said, 'Meena *bhabhi*, problem *nathi*. His passport is with you na? He will not go anywhere. Calm down. He will come back.' He then went back to sleep. Meena bhabhi called him again in the morning, she sounded very excited this time.

'Ramesh bhai, guess what? Papa Matondo is back. He met a Congolese man on the streets in Brussels and he decided to visit his house. He accompanied him to the downtown area where many Congolese people live. He got drunk there and slept the night.' Meena *bhabhi* always called him on some pretext or other, but he knew that all she wanted was to know about her husband's activities.

'Ramesh *bhai. Kem cho*?' she would politely ask, and then she would start rambling on about something or the other. 'You know, I have joined a baking school and discovered the magic of cooking. I go for long walks and meet interesting people.' Then, she would wait for some information about her husband. Ramesh never said much, because he didn't want to upset her in her delicate situation.

She finally delivered a healthy baby boy. Ramesh called her to congratulate her.

'Ohh, he is a delight, Ramesh *bhai*. He coos and gurgles. I finally have someone other than my father that I can call my own. I lost my mother when I was very young. I want a real family now,' she said.

Meena and the baby returned to Kinshasa. A few months later she was pregnant again. She confided in Ramesh that she was more than happy to go back to Brussels.

Another baby boy followed.

Ramesh noticed that since Meena *bhabhi* had two boys, one after the other, she was busy and less nagging. He was happy for her. All her time was now dedicated to raising the boys. Whenever she found time for herself, she drank exquisite wine; practiced yoga; and indulged in buying super expensive designer bags and clothes from exclusive boutiques of Europe. He got Meena *bhabhi*'s updates from her driver.

Ramesh witnessed high life at close quarters. He couldn't even imagine having this kind of a lifestyle. His wife was always struggling in the kitchen, and was always stressed about the children and their rising school fees. She had two pairs of *Punjabi* and one *maxi* that she rotated on a daily basis. Her hair was turning grey, but she had no time to apply *henna* like the other ladies. She was always worried about basics in life. His colleagues faced the same problem. Ramesh's children were attending Mother Teresa School, which followed the Indian curriculum and had been set up by nuns from India. The school fee was $20 per child. Most Indians who worked in shops and other small businesses, sent their children to this school. Their perennial transport problem was solved, when a Punjabi lady rented a small bus and started a bus service for that school. His world thrived on *jugad*. In Ramesh's world, money, food and comfort were always lacking. When he met his counterparts, they shared their misery. But he knew that he would not keep living like this for long. He had been exposed to another world, and now he wanted to be a part of that circle.

Meena *bhabhi* would invite him to visit her at her home, during the rare afternoons when most of the staff were not around. She would entertain him with stories of her friends. Then, she would gently ask about her husband, 'So what's up with Lucky eh?' If he'd been badly treated by his boss that day he would drop a few nasty hints, otherwise Ramesh would say nothing. He genuinely loved her as a sister, and didn't want to psychologically disturb her. It wasn't her fault that she had married a complicated, cold bastard. Ramesh genuinely hated rich people, but Meena *bhabhi* was kind and vulnerable. She was the only one who treated him with respect. Lakha *bhai* didn't even look in his direction.

Ramesh was working very hard at his company and the business was making sizeable profits. One evening after Ramesh finished giving his daily update to Lakha *bhai*, he made a smart suggestion.

'*Patron*, let's start a water purification plant. There is a lot of money to be made in this area. The mineral water available in the supermarkets are so expensive, and there are not many cheap local options. It is a market waiting to be explored.' He looked expectantly at Lakha *bhai*, and waited for him to respond. But Lakha *bhai*, who was going through his messages on his phone, didn't even bother to look up from his desk.

'Ramesh you should focus on our transport business. Timber is a big business right now. Order more *camion*s. Our old trucks are useless. Also right now a lot of money is to be made from timber. You can shut the door after you,' Lakha *bhai* said, and went back to using his blackberry phone. Ramesh walked to the door and opened it.

Suddenly, he turned around and said, 'Lakha Bhai, *tamey khabar che ney.* Green Peace is increasing its pressure on the government. They might come down heavily on timber companies. I'm sure your "white" friends must have informed you.'

Lakha *bhai* clenched his teeth and barked, 'Increase the number of *camions*,' and went back to messaging. Ramesh bumped into Marc, Lakha *bhai's* Lebanese distributor, as he opened the door.

'*Ca va, mon frere* Ramesh?' They touched their heads three times as per the local tradition.

'*Ca va un peu,*' Ramesh laughed.

'I overheard your conversation with the *faux blanc,*' Marc said, as he pulled Ramesh aside. 'He has no vision. I am ready to invest in a water purification plant. And I'll also get two boys from my village to help out. You can arrange for the rest. We'll make good money!' he continued.

'Done deal! *Mon frere*!' I know a Chinese supplier who exports the machinery. And Me? I am king of customs. No problem. Let's launch together.' Ramesh was excited.

Over the next few days Ramesh made a few phone calls, met a few people and greased a few palms. Soon they were manufacturing small sachets of portable water, and selling them for 50 and 100 *Francs* on the street. Both Marc and Ramesh were now making good money on the side. "Congo is complicated. All the big transactions are done in dollars. But no one accepts one dollar notes. All small amounts are paid in Congolaise Francs," Ramesh thought.

'Money brings money, *mon frere*!' Ramesh said, to his business partner Marc. One day, Marc and Ramesh were driving to the water purification plant to carry out an inspection, when they noticed a young Chinese man selling their water in the *marche.*

'*Mai mai mai moins cher,*' shouted the Chinese.

'*Mai mai mai…moins cher,*' imitated Ramesh and laughed. 'Marc, you will see one day I will be patron.'

'*Oui, Boni patron*,' Marc said, and laughed.

The daily newspapers usually carried articles about rebel soldiers in the East, or Vice President Jean-Pierre Bemba's activities. But these days it was the timber industry that was making news. The government was keeping a close eye on the illegal felling of Ebony and Wenge. Both types of wood were in high demand, in South East Asia. Matadi port was flooded with timber containers. The exporters were spinning money. Not anymore. Ramesh felt happy when he read the newspaper reports about how the government was putting a lot of pressure on the timber industry. Green peace was up in arms. Times were tough and Lakha *bhai* was in a bad mood. He was snapping at people more that he usually did.

'*Mon frère*, Marc. Remember how I told that *faux blanc,* Lakha *bhai* about the Green Peace *lafda*. But, motherfucker thinks he is a mister know-it-all. *Lo bhai, dhando pathi gayo. Ab maa chudao. Saala harami.* The timber business is finished in Congo. Go fight Green Peace now,' Ramesh said to Marc. They were getting ready to set up their second water-purification plant, this time in the industrial area.

Ramesh didn't hear much from Meena *bhabhi* anymore, but he knew that she was very busy.

It was a regular bright and breezy day. The Congo River was dazzling under the golden African sun. The fishermen were busy rowing their slim *piroques*; while powerboats zipped through the water, as they transported passengers from Brazzaville to Kinshasa. The Congo River port was busy as always. It was business as usual, as workers loaded and off-loaded bales of African fabric, timber and scrap metals. The local fishermen brought in fresh river fish and carried back dry fish. Ramesh tried to cover his nose as he walked through the port. The stench was terrible. The cleaners were on a strike, as they hadn't received their salaries for three months. He had an appointment with a customs inspector at 11 a.m., and he was already late. He was walking and arguing with another customs official, who had come to their office to inform them of some new tax rules. His phone rang. He was about to ignore it, but then he saw Meena *bhabhi's* name flash across the display screen.

He quickly answered it, '*Jai Shri Krishna, bhabhi*!'

'Ramesh *bhai*, leave everything and come and have breakfast with me,' she insisted. She sounded sad and he couldn't refuse her invitation.

'*Pappa*, don't trouble my men here. You keep me happy and I'll keep you happy,' he told the customs officer, and rushed out.

The traffic was crazy on *Boulevard du 30 Juin*. Chinese workers were digging the road, breaking the divider and cutting the solid old trees that lined the boulevard. Flame of the forest, Jacaranda, Ylang Ylang and other flowering trees were hacked to the ground. The Kinshasa Golf course, a green oasis once hidden by these massive trees, lay exposed. The Chinese company had imported palm trees from China to replace the giant old trees. '*Boulevard du 30 Juin* to look like a road in Dubai!' screamed one newspaper headline. It was a huge mess. The Chinese workers had parked the digger and road roller, bang in the centre of the street. Broadening the existing boulevard was causing nuisance to everyone.

He reached his boss' penthouse around noon and ran up the stairs. He hated taking the elevator after having gotten stuck, in many of them, several times. "Never take the lift if you can climb the stairs in Kinshasa," he would advise everyone.

A maid opened the door and asked him to go to the terrace. Meena *bhabhi* was sitting on an imported rattan sofa, dressed in a flowing white kaftan, with a white turban glamorously wrapped around her head. She was wearing her trademark bright red lipstick and Tom Ford sunglasses.

'She has changed so much, I can't blame her, anyone would go mad living with that bastard, Lakha *bhai*. He is lucky to have a wife like her. But he has destroyed her,' he thought. A slim long vogue dangled from her lips, and half a bottle of Laurent Perrier champagne lay in the champagne bucket in front of her. She picked up the bottle and poured the bubbly into a Lalique crystal flute. She was staring into the vast expanse of the Congo River. Several barges with SUVs parked on them were floating on the water. The skyline of Brazzaville was hazy because of the cloudy June sky. Ramesh cleared his throat. She looked up at him and smiled.

'*Besi jao*, Ramesh *bhai*,' she said, as she pointed to a chair opposite the sofa. She poured him a drink as he sat down.

'I will have *masala chai*, if you don't mind *bhabhi*. I have to go to the *Douanne* from here,' he said. There was an uncomfortable silence. Ramesh shifted in his chair and decided to break the awkward silence.

'*Bhabhi*, you should be in Bollywood movies. You look so beautiful. *Ekdum* slim and trim. You have maintained yourself very well. I am sure the other *bhabhi jis* are jealous of you,' Ramesh joked. Meena laughed so hard that the champagne fell out of her mouth.

'Sorry, Ramesh *bhai*. I'm extremely sorry. Here take some *papier mouchoir* and wipe your face,' she said, as she handed him some tissue paper. It was evident that she was drunk. Ramesh sat in her balcony quietly, while she spoke her heart out. It was all so surreal. He had never imagined a world like this. Kinshasa had two worlds – the sad and miserable world of the poor, and the enchanted life of the rich.

'Ramesh *bhai*, it has been a long journey for me. I have come a long way, from a shy Delhi girl to a Kinshasa wife. Who would have thunk?' she laughed.

'I was studying in Jesus and Mary College, spending time with my father; and now I am part of this crazy and complicated world.' Mamma Patty, the old maid brought a cup of *masala chai* and two Marie biscuits on a tray. Meena *bhabhi* waited for her to leave. She lit another cigarette and carried on with her rant.

'Ramesh *bhai*, this city is something else. The whole world thinks Africa is a dark continent. There are people who think that Africa is a country, they don't even know that it is a continent. Some people now know Nigeria and South Africa! You know my friends in Delhi actually think that we live in huts!' She laughed, and then continued.

'Someone in New York asked me if we have animals roaming in our backyards. They have no clue what our reality is like. Stupid, ignorant people. They don't know we live like royals in Kinshasa. These Kinshasa men are very clever. They are business men after all. It's in their blood. They have become like Congolese businessmen. Haven't you noticed how they eat *fufu*, *pondu* and *liboke* at Mamma Colonel. They can't live without the *pili pili*. But it's a delicate fish bowl and we are like gold fish. Trophy wives, we are nothing but trophy wives! The beautiful bubble that the men have created to keep their wives in this city, with them. I can see through it all. I am educated, Ramesh *bhai*. I understand. It wasn't easy initially, but I understand completely now. These women used to be nice before they got into charity and meditation mumbo jumbo. They are completely brain fucked now. They fly to places like Dubai just to shop and go to the Seychelles Islands whenever they feel like. Now that Joburg boasts of good plastic surgeons, it has become the new hot spot to get a gallon of botox, health check-up, therapists and shopping. This lifestyle is like a drug, you gradually get addicted to it. To tell you the truth, I never believed in Juju, *jadoo tona* and magic. But honestly, after living here I have started to believe in it. You know more about this than I do.'

'Did you not hear about Bilal uncle's son leaving his new born baby and wife of 2 years, for an Air Gabon airhostess? And what did she do? After six months of drama, she ran away with all his money. Now he wants to go back to his wife and child. I hear he hangs out more with the *maulana* at the mosque now than with the girls at nightclubs. What *dramabaazi.*' She excused herself and went to the bathroom.

She returned a few minutes later and Ramesh pushed a bottle of Evian in her direction.

She finished the small bottle and continued, 'Tell me, what do all the wives do here? There is nothing much for them to do – the stay at home wives. Their cooks manage their kitchens, while their children are looked after and assisted by nannies. So what do the wives of leading businessmen actually do?' She was getting excited and the pitch of her voice had increased.

'I will tell you the truth. They entertain themselves by organizing lunches, picnics and charity events. The competition among them is intense and crazy. You can't even imagine how bitchy and catty they can get.' She opened another bottle of Evian and finished it. Ramesh sat quietly without saying anything. He knew he had a lot of work pending, but he felt sorry for Meena *bhabhi*, and waited for her to finish her story. Honestly, he was intrigued. Her rant sounded like something from *Hello* or *Ok*! magazine that he read while waiting at the Belgian doctor's chamber. He could never afford the $50 consultation fee that the doctor charged. But, ever since he had helped him clear his container at the port, the doctor treated him for free.

Meena *bhabhi* let out a loud sigh and continued, 'There is so much competition among the Asian wives here. They compete over things like, who has more white guests attend their party. Seriously, this obsession of hanging out with white people escapes me. Did you know that most of these white people don't even have servants back home? They actually clean their own toilets. And look at them, how they become all fancy here. We give them too much importance. My friend who works in the Belgian embassy here, cleans her house before her cleaner comes in, because she doesn't want him to think that she is messy.' She burst out laughing.

'But we brown people are so obsessed with them. Who speaks or doesn't speak good French? They also compete in wearing the latest fashion from Europe. Watches, bags and jewellery. They are desperate to acquire the top of the line *noveau* collectibles from crockery to jewellery.'

The old nanny brought in a plate of carrot and cucumber sticks with hummus, and set it down on the table.

'*Merci*, Mamma…' she whispered. Ramesh noticed her hands tremble, as she scooped up the hummus with a carrot stick. He looked at her carefully, and realized that she looked very thin and old. However, her forehead had no lines and she had a strange smile plastered on her face. Gone was the fresh and beautiful Meena *bhabhi*. She now looked like a strange plastic doll that constantly wore a surprised expression.

'Rich people always have a full kitchen, but never have the appetite. Whereas, poor people have nothing and are always hungry,' he thought, to himself and smiled. Suddenly, he noticed the time. He had a rendezvous at the customs, but Meena *bhabhi* wouldn't stop talking. She was a genuine person stuck in a plastic world. He decided to stay on and listen to her.

'Rich people get caught up in their fancy problems. While us poor people just rot like garbage on the streets. No one wants to touch us. Our open wounds only fester and then one day we die. Even in death these *haramis* want us to report to work,' Ramesh thought as he absentmindedly tapped his right foot against the ground. He didn't want to be a poor servant anymore. Time was running out. He had to make money. He had to become a *patron*. His resolve was stronger than ever.

He decided to break free from the 'worker mindset' by asking, '*Bhabhi,* can I have another cup of *chai?* Strong please! I don't like the weak tea bag variety.' Meena rang a bell and Mamma Patty came running out. 'You look like a nurse with your hair covered in that white surgical cap and green overalls and a white apron on top,' Ramesh teased her. 'This is my uniform, *Monsieur* Ramesh,' scolded Mamma Patty.

'*Amenez en tasse masala chai avec du lait. En coca* light *bien froide pour mois, sil vous plait,*' Meena *bhabhi* said to her.

He noticed that rich people eat and drink everything 'lite' – lite butter, lite milk and coke light. 'Why look like a refugee when your bank account can feed a poor country's starving population?' he wondered.

Meena *bhabhi* had gone silent. He noticed that she had hardly touched the plate of salad and hummus. She checked her phone and adjusted her turban. Mamma Patty came back with hot *chai* and chilled coke. They both sipped their drinks in silence.

'Hey, have I told you about the famous *Monsieur* Antoine Jaques?' she asked him. She was very animated now. "No, *bhabhi*" responded Ramesh.

'Most of the wealthy wives in Kinshasa vie for the exclusive attention of Antoine Jaques. He is a Belgian Jeweller; and whenever he visits he brings exclusive jewellery, bags and watches to sell. The contents of his patent Louis Vuitton *valises,* causes a social crisis. You should see the way my so-called friends fight with each other just to host him. That clever old man always stays at his old Congolese friend's house by the river, and never with any client.'

She paused and then continued, 'Whenever he is here, these women organize a tea party, and let Antoine display his latest diamonds and watches from Europe. The women go through his collection, and constantly 'ooh' and 'aah' as if in orgasm, while sipping French wine; and purchase like they would buy *arachide*. The price tag doesn't matter, all they want is to show off to each other and make each other jealous.' Meena *bhabhi* stopped to laugh.

'It sounds crazy, right?' She didn't wait for Ramesh to respond, and continued talking.

'I won't lie to you. I am obviously an integral part of this charmed circle and often host a *Prive* – a private viewing for my ten closest confidantes. I always tell them to arrive before the invited guests, so that they can pick out the best pieces. Others casually walk in and sigh, coo and indulgently look at the leftover pieces of jewellery, watches and bags. *Monsieur* Antoine has known *Bapuji*, my father-in-law, for many years now. They are good friends. He treats me like a daughter just because he respects *Bapu ji* so much. *Monsieur* Jaques has made a fortune over the years by catering to the fancy and extreme whims of these ladies. He is both hated and loved by the community because he gets them "Limited Editions" of everything including watches and bags. But they have to pay a huge price for them.'

"He is also a tattletale, and will often reveal scandalous information about the men who refuse to pay him. *Bapu ji* told me that once after having had a few drinks, *Monsieur* Antoine let his guard down and told him about all his clients, and how they make him run before they ultimately pay. These people are *kanjoos*, I tell you!' Meena *bhabhi* said.

'Sorry to interrupt you *bhabhi*, but I have to go. Lakha *bhai* is calling me,' Ramesh said, and offered her an apologetic smile.

'Trust Lucky to spoil my afternoon. Go if you must Ramesh *bhai*. Goodbye,' she said, and got up and walked inside.

Ramesh looked at the huge balcony, he felt like he was on a movie set. A gentle breeze wafting from the Congo River was blowing against his face. Since he was alone, he grabbed the opportunity to walk to the edge of the balcony to get a better view. He looked down at the shimmering, ribbon-like road that ran parallel to the river. It had no potholes, and no litter; it was absolutely clean. Opposite the river, on the other side of the road, lay the palatial embassy residences.

'This is how the rich and privileged live. The regular poor people don't even know this road exists. Who has the time to cycle or jog by the riverside road, after work?' he thought. He enjoyed the panoramic view.

Ramesh spotted three white women in tight gym clothes, running along the side of the road. He did not understand, why they tied a small wrap skirt around their waist. As they ran, the wrap flapped up and down in the breeze presenting a full view of their small, tight butts.

'They don't have much to hide, and they certainly are not my type. I like women who have firm breasts and bootylicious – total value for money. Business is business,' he smiled.

He watched as five little children squealed, as they rode their tricycles, with their nannies chasing after them. Another nanny who was slightly older, was walking behind them with a picnic basket. She was shouting at them to slow down. A white man dressed in a suit and tie was walking with a laptop in his hand. Not too far from the man, a group of a dozen Chinese people were standing and taking pictures in front of the Chinese embassy. Two CD cars zipped past. He could see some *gendarmes* stop the fishermen on their *piroques* and snatch fish from them. Two women clad in *liputa* were planting spinach in the little grove at the bend of the river. A blue convertible car, zipped pass them, blaring loud music. Suddenly, everything came to a standstill as two screeching motorbikes appeared on the road. Ramesh instantly recognized them as belonging to the presidential guards. And then, just like Ajay Devgan in *Phool aur Kante*, President Kabila appeared behind them on a motorbike, and overtook them.

'*Arre saala*!' Ramesh exclaimed, he couldn't believe his eyes. He was watching the president of DRC drive down the road on his Harley Davidson. His guards were running behind him, followed by twenty Land cruisers and a white Mercedes ambulance. Ramesh's phone started to beep. He looked at it and saw that he had a message from Lakha *bhai*. 'Report to head office urgently,' the message stated. Ramesh left and headed to his office. On the way he played and replayed Meena *bhabi's* words in his head. He was intrigued by the world of the rich, and wanted to be rich.

That was the last time he spent alone time with Meena *bhabhi.*

He knew from the driver's updates that Meena *bhabhi* was busy. First she got busy with setting up her dream home, and filled it with expensive things. Then she occupied herself by becoming a gracious host, and constantly had the driver and the nanny running between Pelouse Store, the City Market and Patisserie Nouvelle. She spent her time, in acquiring little treasures. And for every disappointment that she suffered, she bought something to reward herself. Soon, she learned to enjoy the attention she received while hosting her famous lunches and teas. She flew in seafood from Pointe Noire for a special dinner on the balcony. When things got rough and she felt like she needed a breath of fresh air, she would head to Brussels. Thankfully money was never a problem for her, and she spent it with a vengeance. Lakha *bhai's* accountant often spoke about her private expenditure with awe.

Meena *bhabhi* was also the chief patron of three charities, just like her father-in-law. She loved the fact that her charity work and donations made a difference in the lives of people who were suffering. In the meanwhile, Lakha *bhai* remained busy with building and expanding his business empire. Congo was his playground and he bent every rule to maximize his profits.

Meena *bhabhi* finally moved to Brussels permanently, after she discovered that Lakha *bhai* was having an intense affair with his Indian manager's wife. Ramesh had been there to witness the whole thing, and would often recall that day's event to anyone who was interested in listening.

'Uff! What a *tamasha bhabhi ji* created that day.' He chuckled.

'The old horny devil! He deserved every bit of the insult she hurled at him, in every language she knew. Meena *bhabhi* had let loose; she was like a woman possessed. She called up everybody in her community and informed them of what had happened. The entire incident took place on a Monday morning. Everybody was working as usual in the warehouse, when suddenly a very posh Meena *bhabhi* walked in, and started spewing *gaalis* in Hindi.

'Where is that *haramzaada*, pimp of a manager, Gaurav Kumar?' she yelled. The manager soon appeared in front of her.

'Your wife Sunita is a *saali randi*. You married that cheap prostitute to make extra money didn't you? That is the *jaat* of you poor people. You sent your wife to warm Lakha Bhai's bed didn't you? You will die of syphilis, you *harami ka pilla,*' she yelled. Gaurav started sweating; he fished out a handkerchief from his pocket and kept wiping his forehead repeatedly. He was also blinking incessantly.

'*Bhabhi*, I am sure that there has been a misunderstanding,' he stammered.

'I am not your fucking *bhabhi*. You bloody pimp. If you want money, then you should ask me for it. Don't send your wife for *dhanda*. Ask me for money, but don't pimp your wife,' she screamed. Work came to a complete standstill in the warehouse, and the employees rushed to the manager's cabin to hear what was going on.

Gaurav Kumar could hear his own heartbeat. He couldn't breathe. He was aware that the lower level staff could hear everything Meena *bhabhi* was saying.

He repeated himself, '*Madame* I'm sure it's all a misunderstanding.'

'A misunderstanding?!' She laughed, while wiping the tears trickling down her cheeks. Her voice was choked. She had been crying, you could tell.

'Is that what you call prostitution in your village?' She slapped him hard across his face.

'You are fired, leave now,' she yelled.

Lakha bhai watched the drama unfold through the glass panel of his air-conditioned office. He had never expected his wife to find out, and he certainly hadn't expected her to react like this. The rest of the staff were amused, they knew of their *patron's* roving eye and his weakness for busty brown Indian women. They were glad to see their mean boss being publicly humiliated by his wife. They felt avenged for all the insults that he had thrown at them over the years. 'Serves him right,' was their general reaction.

Lakha *bhai* had the reputation of being a womanizer, but there was no concrete proof as yet. While people gossiped about his affairs, there had never been any evidence to back it up. Ultimately it was his driver who had given him away.

Meena *bhabhi's* driver had taken a day off, and she had a ladies lunch to attend. She called up Lakha *bhai's* driver and asked him to pick her up at noon. "*Madame,* I can't come. *Patron* has instructed me to go pick up another *Madame*." He informed. She summoned the driver home immediately and drove with him to the Grand Hotel, where the other *Madame* was dropped. Meena *bhabhi* entered the hotel, and handed over a crisp $10 note to the receptionist, who gave her Lakha Bhai's room number. She then marched up the marble staircase, with her black Valentino stilettos clicking against the cool white stone. Once she was in the foyer, she stopped in front of a mirror and looked at herself. She was staring at a beautiful, well-coiffed woman who was twirling Chanel pearls. She made a mental note to change the colour of her hair, everyone in her lunch circle was sporting the same sun kissed look. She then opened her Birkin bag, took out a piece of chewing gum and popped it in to her mouth. She took a deep breath and reassured herself. She slowly made her way to room 301. She was just about to knock, when she saw a cleaner coming out of room 302 with his cleaning trolley.

She thrust a $20 note on the cleaner's trolley, and said, '*Ouvre la porte.*' She knew by now that it didn't take much to get what one wanted, provided that one was ready to pay a price for it.

'*Oui, mamma,*' the porter said, before using his master key to open the door.

Meena *bhabhi* stormed into the room. Lakha *bhai* was suckling on Sunita's big breasts while she giggled away. Both of them were stark naked, and oblivious to their surroundings. Meena lunged forward like a tigress, and grabbed Sunita by her hair. She then slapped her hard, right across the face. Lakha *bhai* quickly ran to the bathroom with his clothes.

'Lakshman, what is going on here?' she yelled.

'Calm down, Meena. I can explain everything. This is not what you think. You know that Sunita is a trained beautician right? She was just giving me an Ayurvedic Massage,' he said, as he emerged from the bathroom fully clothed. Meena *bhabhi* picked up Sunita's *salwar kameez* and *dupatta* from the floor, rushed to the window, slid it open and threw it out. She then turned around and slapped her again.

'*Didi*, please don't do this. I am a respectable lady. You can ask everyone,' Sunita pleaded, as she cried hysterically.

Lakha *bhai*, grabbed Meena's arm and said 'Let's go home, Meena. That's enough drama for today.'

'You son of a bitch, I will show you, I am going to call

my father right away. He'll deal with you.' Meena *bhabhi* was possessed.

'What *tamasha* in the hotel, and then later in the community. Everyone was amused and entertained. The city needed some real spicy gossip. Ladies night, gentlemen's night and fancy dinner parties now had a solid topic of conversation.' Ramesh felt a bit better.

'Patron, Lakha *bhai* is a devil, a maniac, he has no respect for anybody. Serves him right. He always humiliates his staff publicly, look at how his wife has humiliated him in the whole town,' he told his co-workers. He had not gotten the opportunity to say goodbye to Meena *bhabhi*, who had left for Brussels immediately with her two sons in tow.

A week after Meena *bhabhi* left, Lakha *bhai* called Ramesh to his office.

'I want to host a unique hunting party for my friends. You have exactly two weeks to put this party together. Call that lazy ass, Papa Andre at my *Ma Campagne* house, and ask him to start cleaning up the house and the garden. I also want him to make sure that the pool is cleaned every alternate day from now on,' he barked. Ramesh noticed that Lakha *bhai* looked happier than he ever had. With his wife away, he was pretty much like a single man again and was free to 'mingle' as much as he wanted to. Kinshasa was teeming with all kinds of women – NGO workers, filmmakers and aspiring musicians.

'These girls are not my type at all. They can be easily taken to bed. I might be loose character, but I'm not characterless,' he often joked about himself. 'These free girls are on a quest and willing to try everything exotic! They are the toast of most parties; they dance, play and enjoy the unreal world. Lakha *bhai* is one of their favourite people to party with. His European sensibilities and Indian hospitality makes him popular' Ramesh thought.

Soon word got around. Everyone wanted an invite to Lakha *bhai's* party in *Ma Campagne*. Preparations were on and the expats were ready. The rich locals had already ordered clothes from Europe for this party.

Ramesh went to give Lakha *bhai* an update about the preparations for the party. When he arrived at his office, he was informed by the receptionist that he would have to wait; as Lakha *bhai* was busy having a conference call with his father and father-in-law. Ramesh stood outside Lakha *bhai's* chamber, and listened in on his conversation with *Bapu ji*, Ramji *bhai*. *Bapu ji* was very upset about Meena *bhabhi's* departure. He missed his grandsons, and hated that his son was single again.

'Are you crazy? Have you completely lost it? I will never remarry. Why would I ever do that? I am not friggin' mad. My assets are exclusively for my two boys and not the girls who chase me for my money. To tell you the truth, I am happy that Meena left. I finely got rid of my nagging wife. I no longer have to deal with confrontations about my so called "stag nights", and constant arguments over my wayward ways. We are both happy in our own worlds, Now leave me alone,' Lakha *bhai* yelled at his father, over speaker phone. Ramesh could see the complete breakdown of communication between his two bosses. Times were tough for the organization.

Ramesh now had to make the impending party his priority. He enjoyed entertainment events that were extravagant, especially when they involved naked girls dancing, loud music and lots of alcohol. But, this party was unique. He was tired of dealing with his control freak boss, who constantly kept on calling him for updates.

'*Saala*, needs a good fuck. He is frustrated and he takes it out on me.' His phone rang. It was Lakha *bhai* again.

'Ramesh, this is my event. You understand? No *lafda*. Make it *ekdum* fine,' he barked.

'*Vanda nathi,* boss. You will see for yourself. It will be the party of the year…' Lakha *bhai* disconnected the call before Ramesh could even complete his sentence.

'*Teri Ma ki*!' Ramesh yelled into his Nokia mobile.

'Its money that gives you the power to misbehave. And one day I will make plenty of it,' he said to himself. He hated being insulted like this every day, but he was a poor man who had to do whatever he could to survive; and the rich took advantage of this.

Ramesh was working overtime to put together the hunting party. Lakha *bhai's* company imported alcohol, so arranging *daaru* was not a problem. The biggest problem he faced right now, was making the arrangements for the antelopes and gazelles to be bought to the property. The highlight of the party was going to be a hunt for the highly elusive Okapi, which Ramesh had somehow arranged to be transported to the farmhouse. A makeshift cage was built for it, and was placed right at the entrance of Lakha *bhai's Ma Campagne* villa. Soon all the arrangements had been made, and the following Saturday the party was underway. The guests were impressed by the lavish and opulent hunting party.

Two trained Bonobos had been put in a cage near the entrance. They waved at the guests as they entered, imitated them and even smoked cigarettes. They drew the biggest crowd 'Bonobos are the closest species to human beings. Go say hello to your grandfather!' Ramesh joked with the guests.

Ramesh knew that this was one party that they would never be able to forget. There were animals all over the vast *Ma Campagne* property. Ramesh had hired African drummers, who were beating their drums as if they were possessed. Fire-eaters stationed at the entrance performed their tricks. The sun was bright. The rays hurt the eyes. The pool water was sparkling blue and looked inviting. The floating bar counter attracted everyone. There were different shades of skin exposed in the pool. The pool was full of women, who were splashing around and drinking champagne; while the men were on the prowl.

The real party started. Rifles were brought out on large platters, and the guests took turns at shooting the animals. It was a barbaric sight. Blood splashed everywhere as everyone cheered loudly. Soon the barbeque was set up to roast the game meat. Lakha *bhai* found Ramesh throwing up in the bathroom.

'Ramesh, there are a few policemen outside. They think that something illegal is going on here, please handle them.'

Ramesh looked at him and said, 'This is child's play for me, *patron*.' Ramesh knew how to handle the policemen, he had been dealing with them for years. He immediately sorted the matter and sat down on the steps to watch the drama.

'This is life boss. This is what money can do to you.' He wanted a dream life like Lakha *bhai's*.

He knew that Lakha *bhai* was a miser by nature. "*Patron* Ramesh, if *Patron* Lakha see our *baguette*s he steal from us and eat them." Many security guards had informed him. 'Money, diamonds, cars and women. I have the bug now. I have to move. Enough of Lakha *bhai's* senile ways. There is no margin for me. Lakha *bhai* is a vampire that sucks money out from everything,' Ramesh thought.

Ramesh knew that it was time for him to move on.

He soon left Lakha *bhai* to join another firm that offered him a higher salary, along with a flat on Avenue Commerce. He was tired of living beyond the squalor Ndjilli Airport. He needed to live in the heart of the business centre, in order to make it big. He was tired of commuting and he was tired of living like a dog.

He had walked into Lakha *bhai's* office a week after the party, and informed him of his decision to quit his present job.

Lakha *bhai* was livid. '*Saala, teri jaat ni,*' he shouted.

'Lakha *bhai*, you are abusing like an Indian. Oho, I forgot, you are a *ranga siyar* yourself. A wolf in sheep's clothing,' Ramesh responded calmly.

'Shut up and get back to work,' bellowed Lakha *bhai*. He paused to take a deep breath and then continued shouting, 'Wait till I get you deported. You can't leave my business in the middle like this. I will report you. I will frame you in a fraud case, cancel your work permit and send you to rot in Makala prison.' Ramesh was seething with anger now. He clenched his fists and moved closer to Lakha *bhai*.

Then he looked him straight in the eye and boldly declared, 'I am leaving your company today. Ask the accountant to settle my account. If you cheat me of even $1, I will talk.' Ramesh then walked out of the office and slammed the door behind him. He fished out a packet of *gutkha* from his pocket, ripped it open and emptied its contents into in his mouth. The fragrant tobacco mix always boosted his confidence. He knew what he was doing. 'I know Lakha *bhai* will beg in front of him. One day…one day…it will happen. I just know it will. I do not know how? when? I know I am going to be the king of Kinshasa. Then all these money sucking motherfuckers will bow down and do *salaam* to me…' he thought to himself.

Metro, Bulot and Beer

Ramesh was fed up of the constant hurdles and challenges life threw at him.

"Look at my life, and look at Lakha *Bhai*'s life. I work hard in the heat, and he enjoys the pleasures of life – sitting in his AC chamber." He despised having to wake up early in the morning and rush to the bus stop to secure a place in the jam-packed *matatu*. The van would load people to double its capacity, and those who couldn't get in were promised by the driver that he would be back soon. Then the mad drive would begin through the narrow by lanes. The driver obviously wanted to maximize his morning profit. He was hardly paid by the bus owner, and he had to make pocket money for himself. The *matatu* driver would swear at every passer-by, knock over small cars, and break the signal. He was like many other *matatu* and taxi drivers, men on a mission. The entire workforce from various quarters from outskirts of the city heads towards Limite, Gombe and beyond. A wave of Congolese work force swarms around for work in the expat occupied area and Marche Centrale.

Everyday Ramesh witnessed a mass of humanity flood into the city to work and by evening it ebbs out, back into the outskirt, into their little niches, just like little secrets tucked away. On the way back the commuters discussed the same problem. He overheard their plight, of how they surreptitiously charge their mobile phones at work and when they are discovered some employers charge them for using electricity. Many cry when a few dollars are deducted from their salaries, for charging their phones at work.

Someone mimicked their master, Electricity bills are expensive '*Ca coute cher*. Why you charge your phone here. I will take away $5 from your salary.' The commute back home was easy to deal with, despite the heat and lack of space, because of these stories.

'Our poor neighbourhood has little electricity or running water. Where do we charge our phone?' asked one middle-aged man. 'And they expect you to answer your phone on the first ring.' Everyone nodded in agreement.

'Today, I was accused and insulted for stealing two bottles of water,' said a young woman.

Another young girl, almost sitting on her lap said, 'You spit in her water tomorrow. OK? I always spit in my *madame's* food.'

'Eh! *Zoba*!' an old man scolded her. She stuck her tongue out at him.

'This morning, my *matatu* broke down and I reached Gombe at 7 a.m. My *Madame* was screaming like a mad woman.' The children are almost ready for school. You lazy mamma, always sleeping. Wake up early if transport is a problem. I wanted to tell her that I wake up 4:30 in the morning. She deducted $5 from my $80 salary.' Everyone sighed, too tired from work.

Ramesh liked the Congolese, they were a hardworking and happy lot. They were ready to face life's challenges every morning. He felt sorry for the vendors who carried fruits and vegetables to be sold, and goats to be slaughtered. They always preferred to sit on the *matatu* top. The top of the van offered enough space for them and their goods, and they could breathe. Finding a place inside the *matatu* and keeping ones self-inside, was a fine art mastered by the *kinoise*.

He was always amazed by the local Congolese girls dressed like models in their bright dresses and high heels, beautiful make up, elaborate hair do, going out into the city to look after white people's children. The '*nounous*' or nannies.

They could speak a smattering of English, had expensive phones and nice bags. After all rich people's children loved them. He knew that the *madames* tolerated them because the *nounous* ran the house. The *nounous's* conversation fascinated him, because they always discussed the private lives of their *madames* in the minivan. He would squeeze in next to the ladies to overhear the gossip. It was mostly the same story but new spices every day.

"*Madame* went to the gym, attended lunch, tea, mani-pedi – hair appointments." "*Madame*'s best friend is very jealous of her. She bought the same bag as my *madame*." "*Madam*e had a fight with the patron after she went through his phone." "*Madame* is taking too many pills, she is nervous." "*Madame* has a secret lover." The nannies pacified, cleaned, bathed, sang and fed the kicking, crying and colic babies. Some days had real masala story, like the *patron,* eyed the gentle arch of her back or the swell of her breast, and the nanny was instantly kicked out. The other nannies heard from their *madame* that the '*Madame*' went to town crying about the loss of 'ungrateful' help. The nannies exchanged similar notes. They noted everything while serving drinks and snacks. While their *madames* cluck clucked tsked and consoled the 'hurt *madame*' over tea.

It would become a joke over party afters, 'I told you, she is so insecure.'

'I knew her husband has a roving eye.'

'That's her middle class background. She can't groom herself like us. Clink of diamonds and Noritake cups, a bit of cupcake and laugh over the loss of a nanny. Complicated world of the rich and Ramesh wanted to be a part of it.

The *matatu* rides would always make Ramesh sick and queasy. However, he always tried to distract himself by talking to others. Today, he was sitting next to a young Sindhi man who had just arrived from Pune, and was working in a shop. The young man was ready to faint in the *matatu*. Ramesh tried to distract him.

'*Bhau*, you like them eh? The Congolese girls keep themselves "tip top", *nahi*?' Ramesh nudged the young man sitting next to him.

'I am sure they dream of one day living in a house just like their *patron*'s. You never know, with so many *chutiya goras* running riot in Kinshasa in a quest to discover Africa, they might marry these nounous!' the young boy laughed. Ramesh continued, 'Some have good *kismet*. In fact my neighbour, a beautiful girl of sixteen, blessed with a figure like a model, would sing at the Piano Bar. What did the neighbours say? "Aaah she looks like Naomi Campbell, she makes good money with all the white guys tipping her generously and getting pictures clicked with her, to post on Facebook. The smart girl soon discovered their motive, now she charges 5 dollars straight (no negotiations) if you want a picture with her hugging you. *Saali*, one *chalu cheeze* she is. Never gave me any *patta*. Prostitute *besharam*. Naomi Campbell my foot. One day, I will get the real one to Kinshasa! I will show them!" His favourite refrain now, 'I will show them!' The young man wasn't paying any attention now. Ramesh poked him.

'Best part of the story, now she is married to an old British diplomat and the poor old chap has opened a small boutique of party clothes for her in Gombe. Every girl aspires to achieve what she has.' He laughed.

'*Bichari*, trying so hard, with the padded bra and swinging hips. *Chalo*, let them find a *chutiya gora*!'

The young man had slept off on his shoulder. As the broken brown *matatu* rattled down, like a manic monster out to eat the whole town and clear it of its own ugliness; now he could barely hold himself from vomiting right there on everybody's sticky-with sweat backs. He was trying hard to keep calm. His eyes fell on the deep cleavage of a woman sitting next to him, and he could now predict the pattern of the trickling sweat drops, meandering down from the multi-coloured braids to her face, falling from her cheeks, from the edge of her cheek bone down, to her neck, and finally into the deep valley of her breasts. The bold flowers printed around the heaving breasts were watered from her own sweat. Gradually the entire foundation on her face was washed off by the awful sweat. The entire make up was washed off.

'Such a waste of effort,' he thought. But, the woman was not cowed down; she managed to pull out a serviette from her bag after nudging a few passengers, and wiped her face, but could not clean her neck. There was no space. She dabbed her face a second time after folding the serviette, now wet with sweat. It exposed a better face, a face of a young girl unsure, vulnerable in her own poverty. She was still untouched by the fine lines that often provide ridges for the foundation to settle in. But hers was a supple skin, a skin that screams teenage. She was trying her best to raise her hand and wipe her face again, but there was just no space for her to move. Thank God that there was enough oxygen for everyone to breathe, often passengers got breathless and fainted. This caused so much distress and anger among the passengers; no one wanted to be late for work. Today, thankfully no one fainted. They somehow manage to report to their *bulot* on time.

Ramesh was getting late for his appointment with Sona *bhai*. He did not want him to think that he was lazy, for these days there were far too many *chokros* fresh from the villages in Gujarat, who were willing to work for much less. They were spoiling the whole business market by accepting low salaries and shared accommodation. He didn't want to lose this opportunity.

Rich people living in AC houses, driving AC cars, never understood 'transport' problem. All they could do is scream at their workers for being lazy, and often deduct their salaries.

Change is the Only Constant

Ramesh sort of knew the timid Sona *bhai,* his soon to be boss. He would often come across him at the river port, or very rarely in the bars in the evening. It was Sona *bhai* who sent him a private message, proposing a job offer in his yet to take off enterprise. The whole town was talking about his fall out with Lakha *bhai.*

Sona *bhai* dealt with sundry items. He imported containers from China and filled it with electronics, bicycles, furniture, electric fittings, etc. The imported goods were 'brand less'. Sona *bhai* had the sticker of all the popular electronic brands. He had a special glue gun and he stuck the brand stickers on the products, based on the demand of the customers. No one on Avenue Commerce had caught on to this idea till now. He had every brand available at a much cheaper rate as compared to the showroom prices. Sona *bhai*'s shop in Avenue commerce always buzzed with customers. When customers walked in, they saw the display and once they made up their mind, the brand sticker was quickly stuck on the product, in the depot behind the shop, and made ready for delivery. New and smart version of television, DVD players, and fridges were much in demand. He was minting money in the electronic retail business. But his wife, the sharp and far sighted businesswoman knew that they have to diversify, because everyone now brought a container from China and sold it in Avenue de Commerce. Very soon every shop on Avenue Commerce will sell fake electronics. The trick was to think ahead and she was forcing Sona *bhai* to foray into the construction business. Sona *bhai* had also heard that because of the new boom in construction, iron nails will be in big demand and wanted to set up a small factory to produce iron nails. He could see the United Nations trucks and Land Cruisers grow in number on the streets of Kinshasa. MONUC people were renting apartments and paid very good rent. They were plenty now and many more were rumoured to come. Expats and locals were tired of living in villas, they wanted to move into luxurious apartments. New building projects were coming up. Sona *bhai* had to do something different and his wife was constantly pushing him. She somehow knew everything that went around in that town, before him.

Sona *bhai* knew that Manikchand was the man who could help him pull through the new business. Manikchand was a *harami*, but he had a way with business in this part of Africa.

'Business in Francophone West Africa was very different from East Africa.' Sona *bhai* always said.

'You see my cousin has a small business in Uganda. Margins are less but life is easy. Tanzania, Uganda and Kenya use simple and easy to handle. Models. Though things changed a lot there too. It's not the same land where our Indian ancestors landed and traded with the Arabs and locals. It was easy back in those days, in East Africa. The Indians set up shops, later small factories, often married a local woman and maintained a half-caste family. It was all good till it lasted but not anymore. Things started to change after a strong wave of nationalization that swept the not so new, independent countries. The business environment was different, the Indian traders were targeted, their shops often vandalized. They lived under a threat of random attacks. Many families started moving to West Africa.' Sona *bhai* always said the same thing. He had learnt English in Congo and often mixed up the tenses.

'In West Africa the Gujaratis, Ismailis and Sindhis miss the big *jamatkhana* of Dar es Salaam, or the *chai* and *jalebi dukas* of Mombassa. *Dhanda* is difficult in West Africa, but the profit is staggering. If you hit the right *dhanda* here, life will be set. Lingala is not a difficult language to learn. French is of course difficult and used mostly by the *patrons*.' Sona *bhai* was trying to hold a polite conversation with Ramesh. Sona *bhai* grudgingly admired Ramesh, who with his glib tongue in Lingala and Gujarati, and a sharp mind could do anything. He needed proper guidance though, thought Sona *bhai*, and he could be an asset. Sona *bhai* made a lucrative offer. Ramesh, jobless jumped at this offer with a raise in salary, better housing and percentage share in new business.

Ramesh demanded a 5 per cent share in the new timber business that Sona *bhai* wanted to start. Timber and scrap trading were money-spinners. There was a lot of money to be made. So much scrap lay around, but you needed someone like Ramesh to pull it off. Sona *bhai* agreed to employ Ramesh and offer him 4 per cent share in the timber and scrap business.

Sona *bhai* and his wife ran their business like sharks. *Madame* Sona *bhai* was the real boss. People called her "*Mamma Mobulu*," or "*Femme Terrible*" or "*Femme de la Marche*". She screamed and shouted at the workers, including the boys from her village. There was no question of getting business on credit if she was in the shop. She had no time for people who strolled into their shop for a casual chat or *chai*. She was a control freak and knew how to crack the whip. Sona *bhai* had no or little say when she was around, and everyone knew how much he feared her.

Today, *Madame* Sona *bhai* did not come to the shop. Ramesh was instructed to drop the day's collection at Sona *bhai's* house. It wasn't a big amount, but it would be a good loyalty test for him. He reached their house with the packet of cash. The cook made him wait in a small room next to the Salon. The curtain was not drawn properly, and he could watch as *bhabhi ji* entertained her group of friends. He stood there watching these women show off their new dresses, jewellery and blow-dried hair. He could overhear their conversation, and it was the same conversation one heard in restaurants, bars, and the *mandir* and the mosque. Sona *bhai's* wife and her friends were complaining about the local staff being lazy and slow.

'These stupid workers. Always come up with the same excuse. *Madame* transport problem. *Arre bhai*, do something *na*? Wake up early. Be sincere. I have threatened to throw them out of the job. At least it will make them less lazy.'

Another woman in a tight red and black dress popped a *samosa* in her mouth, and spoke while eating, 'Have you noticed the way they look at you when you eat. And they are always in a rush to leave after 4:00 p.m. I say, hey you! Look at my Rolex, it shows perfect time. Its 3:30 p.m., and their behaviour changes. They become slow with ironing the clothes or watering the plants. And want to run away after 4:00 p.m. Oh! *Madame,* transport problem,' she mimicked. She wiped her face with a wet towel. Actually she had bought this very expensive pack of 'Olay face refreshing towelettes' from Joburg, South Africa; and wanted her friends to notice that she no longer used the regular tissue paper, but the latest 'use and throw' scented wet wipes.

She continued, '*Arrey*! Who will make *chai* for me and give milk to the *children*. I don't like *chai* stored in the thermos. It has to be sipped *garam-garam*. Why are you here, *baba*? I *toh* tell them right on their face, think of a new new *bahana*, what *ghisa pita* excuse? No transport? Eh.'

She popped another *samosa* and started to discuss the extra marital affairs shown on TV. 'Look what is happening in India, *tauba! Tauba!* No morals left in our country. I am so glad that we can keep an eye on our husbands here.' She was really getting excited. Ramesh was quick to notice that two women winked at each other and smiled.

One tilted her head to expose a brand new diamond solitaire earring, and said in a shrill voice, 'What do you know of your husband's behaviour when he goes to China?'

The other woman giggled, '*Arrey bhai*, forget China, that is far far away. What about when he goes to the port? Matadi is bustling with prostitutes, I have heard. Be careful, these women have magic down there.' They all laughed, a very uncomfortable laugh, for everyone's husbands travelled to Matadi. The woman picked up another *samosa* and warned her friends, before biting into it.

'Leave my husband alone. Watch out for your own. I know everything. My husband comes home to tell me everything including stories about your husbands. Don't force me to open my mouth and spoil Sheila's party.' She seemed angry.

Ramesh was waiting outside the living room, to hand over the packet of cash to Sheila, his boss's wife. But, didn't disturb the interesting conversation of these half-naked women. He was enjoying the full view of their legs and cleavage. He stood there and grabbed a few golden-brown, crisp, onion *bhajiyas* with *pili pili,* as the maid carried it inside for the tea party. She turned around and snatched the second helping, just as he was about to put it in his mouth.

'It's meant for the *Mesdames* and not *shegues* like you,' hissed the middle-aged Carol, under her breath. He pouted his lips and pretended to kiss her. She laughed and pushed him away.

He continued to stand transfixed, taking in the aromas of crisp golden *bhajiyas,* hot brown *samosas, khandvi* and *chai.* His stomach rumbled; he was hungry and there, right in front of his famished face was a continuous train of hot snacks, being carried to the living room from the kitchen. He held his right hand with the left, to stop himself from grabbing something to eat. He was watching *ekdum masaledar* spicy entertainment right there, much better than Zee TV and Sony TV.

'The Indian *bhabhi jis* are now wearing short frocks to show their white, white legs, to everyone,' Ramesh thought. He was busy imagining his ugly boss with his wife.

'Ahhhaa... *Saala* lucky *harami. Mazedar garam-garam biwi* at home. But, who wants a bitch like her?' Ramesh asked himself.

'*Saali,* keeps all the money and gives her husband a daily allowance ... and if she is angry? Oho, then no daily allowance for him, and for lunch he only gets *chapati* and dry potatoes. He keeps her updated on all the business deals. Sheila, the wife, is the brain behind the business and he is only a showpiece. A front man to execute all her plans,' Sona *bhai's* cousin had once told him.

'Ten years ago, she came from a small village in Kutch, no knowledge of Hindi or English. And today she speaks Lingala like a local, and can do *git, pit, git, pit* in English,' thought Ramesh. The whole town knew how she had learnt English from her children, who studied in an English school. She was always confident and smart, but could never understand the English of the white people. Now, her own children spoke like them, the white people. Since she always thought in terms of profit and loss, she would sit attentively with her children to learn, while the tutor came to help them with their homework. Pay for two kids and get services for three! A quick learner, Sheila grasped English fast. She pushed her husband to make more money. They moved their kids from the local English school, to the American International School. She attended high teas and lunches, and spoke in English with her friends. The ladies loved to imitate Sheila, in her absence. They would pout, roll their 'Rrrrs' and speak in an exaggerated American accent, "I have never alloweded my children for sleep over's", "I was borned in India", and "you know, she suicided"; and then they laughed till they teared up. Sheila and her husband were laughed at behind their backs. She was the dictator, while he was the spineless husband. She cracked the whip and he followed her instructions. Ramesh was enjoying his thoughts, while chewing on his *gutkha*.

'This packet is not fresh. The nuts have turned dry and rancid.' *Thooh*, he spat out the brown liquid on Sheila's fluffy white carpet.

He made a mental note to tell the Indian grocer, Naim *bhai* that all the stuff in his shop had either expired or fake. The other day, he bought some sweets and they were all spoilt. The owner's wife had scratched off the date of expiry from all the sweet boxes, and forced every customer to buy them. He laughed again.

'*Saala*, these women know how to make money. My wife can only reproduce. She only knows how to get pregnant, that's it. *Saali*, but she is good at heart.' He was still waiting outside the salon, waiting to handover the bag of cash to Sheila. She was busy showing her new Louis Vuitton bag to her friends.

'It's not a speedy, mind it,' she said, her chin up and heavy breasts swelling with pride. '*Saali*, she has forgotten her past. I remember her when she first arrived in Kinshasa,' thought Ramesh.

Sheila, the newly-wed before, arrived from Porbandar to join her husband, Sona *bhai,* who worked as an accountant in his uncle's electronics shop. Ramesh remembered her being a brash and outspoken woman. There was nothing 'newly-wed' about her. She was bold and used to wear bright transparent nylon saris; and would often visit her husband at his uncle's electronics shop on *Avenue de Commerce.* She was young, beautiful and ready for life in Kinshasa. She managed to sell all her *saris* and *Punjabis* to the local women, within two months of her arrival in Kinshasa. She bought second hand "Western clothes" from the local market with the money.

'I have business in my blood and I can never work under someone. Sona *bhai,* do something *ney?* Let's start small,' she would urge her timid husband.

'Eh, *tamara jaat ni*! My useless husband. I will show you now how to make money. I am opening a ladies beauty parlour from next week,' she informed her husband. 'Good luck, *mahri Hema Malini*!' Sona *bhai* smiled at his wife. He knew that she was a firecracker, and that he did not deserve a strong and beautiful wife like her. But he loved her and always wanted to see her happy.

Sheila spent the next ten days organizing one room in her two-bedroom apartment. The local carpenter quickly made a massage table, two chairs and one big mirror. She dug out portraits of her favourite Bollywood movie stars and put up posters of Madhuri Dixit, Kareena Kapoor and Bipasha Basu. She asked her young Sindhi neighbour to print her price list – "Eye brows $5, eyebrow and upper lips $10. Eyebrows, upper lips and chin $15. Shahnaz Facial $30. Rich feel facial $25."

'*Su fine che*!' She clapped her hands in glee. 'It's the best beauty parlour in town,' she informed everyone in the temple. Sheila *bhabhi* was ready with "Look good beauty parlour."

"I make you look like a new," was her slogan. She started off slow, but with word of mouth her popularity grew. She moved to a small shop on Avenue Commerce where she started selling undergarments, cosmetics and imitation jewellery. The parlour continued to flourish on the first floor of the shop. She invited her cousin from Dar es Salaam to run the parlour, as she was now ready for bigger things. She had finally managed to convince Sona *bhai* to quit his job, and branch out on his own. Together they started importing small containers of sundry items and established their own company.

Madame Sheila finally spotted Ramesh. She yelled, '*Su che*?' And he whispered, 'Cash', and gestured towards the fat envelope. Her facial features softened and she sashayed towards him, as if walking on a ramp. Ramesh enjoyed how the other women made funny faces at each other and exchanged knowing glances, while pointing at her backside.

'She is soo fat…Needs to visit the gym…They jiggle like two stuffed cushions,' the ladies whispered and giggled.

'She should go to Beirut and fix herself, like the Lebanese women do,' giggled one.

Another acquired a serious look and whispered, '*Arre* don't you know? It's better and cheaper in Joburg. Go there do botox *shotox*, shop and come back to Kinshasa.' Sheila could hear them all. She knew their type of women, jealous of her and her husband's success. She swayed her hips even more and walked towards that annoying Ramesh. And he got a full view of her front – nice, jumping breasts. She adjusted the neck and it exposed her wobbly breasts even more.

'Patron sent this for you.'

'OK, you can go now.' She was annoyed with his lechery and made a note to tell her husband never to send this man home. Ramesh continued to stare.

'Woman walking towards you or walking away from, you always see two bouncy balls. Oho, I'm such a *harami*.' He laughed at his own joke. The air conditioner whizzed and it was cool.

'Madame has *mast* first class life. *Thanda, thanda,* cool, cool AC. Nanny, cook, and all she does is give orders. No tension, boss.' Ramesh had to trudge back to work.

Ramesh was lucky to find transport to go back home, right next to Sona *bhai's* house. He ran after the *matatu*, and quickly hopped on and grabbed the conductor's seat. He couldn't stop thinking of Sheila *bhabhi*. From a 'nobody' to a businesswoman, Ramesh had witnessed Sheila *bhabhi's* journey. He thought of his wife, '*Mahri* wife, *eh saali* good for nothing. Only producing children and increasing my headache.'

The crying and shouting of irritating babies, and their harried mothers, in the *matatu,* broke his thoughts. The mothers tried to shove their big breasts in the children's mouths to calm them; and he thought this would calm his mind too. At least he could now look at big breasts for the rest of the way instead of angry, fighting and argumentative Congolese men.

'*Chalo bhai*, one has to learn to adjust in life.' He smiled and stared at all the women for the rest of his journey. His thoughts always drifted to a lavish life – an air-conditioned car, big villa, and swimming pool – just like the patrons'. He deserved it, after all it was his hardwork, and his boss was living off it.

'One day, one day, I will rule this city!' he told himself.

When he had saved some decent amount money, he started to take a shared motorcycle taxi. He was invariably squished between the driver, and a local woman carrying a live chicken in one hand, a huge handbag in the other, with a baby dangling dangerously from her back. The baby was always tied around the back with a bright coloured African cloth. She would try and balance herself on the recklessly driven two-wheeler, by adjusting her big breasts against his back. The chicken would peck the scabs off his eczema-infested legs.

'Ouch! Ouch!' he would yell, but the bird, would be busy pecking on the scabs, leading to more pus oozing out; and soon they would be covered with dust. The big African mama rubbing her big breasts against his puny back, was trying to balance on the Yamaha motorbike. He could feel her taut nipples against his bones; they would poke him, digging deep into him, as if they were making fun of his skeleton like frame against her huge fat wobbly giant body. He had a strange feeling of the bike sinking in the dirt road, with the heavy weight of the big mamma riding behind him. He felt a bit aroused by the constant rubbing of the bodies.

'*Chalo paisa vasool*! I got my money's worth. Some sexual titillation before I start working with the dickheads,' he thought.

In the Name of God

Downtown Kinshasa is dotted with small nightclubs that play good music. Locals and expats hop from one club to another in search of girls, entertainment and business.

Sitting in the expensive "Piano Bar", Ramesh was downing his fourth Mutzig in the company of local girls, conmen and some expats.

'*Pappa, change la chanson*!' he yelled, at the Deejay.

'*Il faut jouet la chancon pour la jeune!*' He laughed and looked at the young girls for approval, but they were busy looking around for new contacts. It was 6 p.m. on a Saturday, and the Piano bar was bursting at its seams. The waitresses dressed in tight black micro miniskirts and super tight white blouses – buttons ready to pop and breasts ready to burst – were skidding on their stilettos serving drinks. They precariously balanced their trays, while being groped and backslapped. Every man wanted to display his contact with the fabulous bar girls, and also make sure that their drinks kept flowing. Tables were full. Conversation was loud, over the extremely loud music and lewd laughs.

Ramesh spotted Rahul, an old acquaintance with some *metisse* men and women. Rahul wore a thick, shiny gold chain, with a big cross hanging from it around his neck. Two gold bracelets jiggled around his wrists, as he emphasized a point with his expensive mobile phone.

'Rahul *bhai*… *Kem cho*? *Ca va*? Long time *bhai*. How are you?' Ramesh yelled from across the bar, and pushed his way through to reach his friend. He spilled a few drinks but was flippant as usual.

'Pardon… Pardon, *ma belle*!… Boss… sorry, eh,' he laughed as he crossed over.

'Rahul *bhai*? You win lottery? Shiny, shiny everything?' winked Ramesh.

'My new name is Raul, Ramesh *bhai* and I'm a Christian now. All change. Everything new! My new English God is making me rich, giving me new brothers and sisters and business. Meet my new family,' Raul introduced him to his companions. Ramesh shook hands with all of them and handed them his card.

'Your English God is a good god Raul brother. He give you *beaucoup* women and plenty money. Keep him. Remember sharing is caring. Where you find your god? How he pay you? He give you girls…Eh, eh,' he winked.

Ramesh's mind was spinning. There was something special about Raul now. He wasn't the same Rahul who had come from Porbandar, ten years ago. A lanky, tall teenager, seventeen years old. He was fair, almost like a girl. He worked for a distant relative in the Commerce Area, and lived with four other guys from his village who all worked in different shops. Ramesh laughed out loud, when reminded of the time when Rahul was raped by his uncle one night.

'*Behenchod*, what scandal. *Sara gaam ma khabar aag mafik phaila.*' The whole town knew of it immediately. Rahul was bleeding badly and was rushed to CMK hospital, on the port of Congo River. Ramesh was at the port, loading timber in containers when he heard the news. He asked the other Indian guy to continue the process, while he rushed to the hospital. There was a big *tamasha* at the hospital. The Congolese doctor was shocked, and threatened to report the matter to the police.

'*Toi, tu est Indien? C'est quoi ca? Je va appelez la* police.' The others present there were relieved to see Ramesh there. He had a natural knack of dealing with such issues.

Ramesh took the doctor aside and spoke to him. The doctor wasn't convinced. Ramesh quickly called Jignesh *bhai* to the hospital. It was after Jignesh *bhai*, the old *patron* and virtual head of the Hindu community intervened, that the matter was sorted out.

'Jignesh *bhai* was Jamesh Bond type. *Ekdum* hero *mafik roab*. Not like *aaj kal ka patron*. He commanded respect,' Ramesh told the others, while Rahul was in the operation theatre.

'Now his sons have taken over the business and he mostly spends his time in Canada. His *chokra log* are no good, only busy chasing these *goris* from the NGO. And these *goris* also are *chalu* type. They will hang out with anybody who offers them free drinks and food. They quickly call their other friends to join in and then *khaya, piya khiska*. They are very smart to make some excuse and disappear. Only sleeping around among themselves. Anyway, they are white trash types; not like those classy white ladies in sleeveless dresses, driving air-conditioned cars. They are my type,' he told them.

'One day,' he promised himself, 'one day I will have one of these society women in bed. Money boss, *paisa, l'argent* can open all doors.'

The same Rahul was Raul today. Raul walked out of the Piano Bar to make an important phone call. Ramesh tailed him. He had to find out more about this rich English god. He was lurking in the corner, while Raul finished his call. The music inside the Piano Bar was thundering; men and women were on the prowl. There was high sexual tension and alcohol flowed. A young Belgian girl, a NGO worker, leaned forward and said something interesting to the middle aged man, an American Peace Corps volunteer. A group of doctors from '*Medicins Suns Frontiers*' were laughing while their eyes were flitting. The local girls were getting impatient; they kept checking their fancy and flashy watches. Someone rolled a joint with precision, eyes vacant, while he tapped his foot to local jazz. You need it to survive in Congo. The drummer, drummed away, as if on a high; his dreadlocks swinging with every beat. An elderly Dutch lady was eyeing him.

'Did she fancy him in bed?' thought Ramesh... 'Aah this place can be so lonely. We all yearn... yearn for that comforting hug; someone's head on our pillow; the warmth of another body breathing in tandem, next to ours.' The drummer opened his eyes and stared right back at the Dutch lady. Ramesh was watching the whole drama unfold right in front of him.

'Will they or will they not?' he thought to himself.

'*Au revoir, merci*!' Raul was ready to leave. Ramesh grabbed Raul's shoulder in the dark.

'*O C'est que ca? C'est qui*?' said a startled Raul.

'*C'est moi*! Ha, ha, ha!' laughed Ramesh.

'*Bhai*, I want to ask you something serious. Where you find this English God? How he make you rich?' asked Ramesh. Raul sensed a deep desperation.

Raul decided to tell all. 'After all I will get more perks for bringing in more converts to my church,' he thought.

'Look Ramesh *bhai*, it's not that simple. Religion is serious stuff and you can't play with it. You can be in trouble if you play truant. There are many local churches run by various groups, some by missionaries, and others by pastors. The local church promises to help the needy, provide education to the children and rehabilitate the new converts. The pastors from Nigeria and Congo have become very strong centres of power. They control the business centres, where most dread to venture. It is here that money and important contacts can be made. Go for it Ramesh *bhai*. But be careful,' warned Raul.

'I am ready, Raul boss.' Ramesh slapped Raul's back. 'I think this is a signal from your English god.'

Raul dialled a number and spoke to someone. 'It's set Ramesh *bhai*. They will call you.'

Ramesh couldn't walk straight that night. His drinks were mixed and he took a few drags of the loaded cigarette. His head was ready to explode. Thankfully, Raul dropped him home.

'Ramesh *bhai*, take care,' Raul shouted, and drove off. Some young Indian boys were still hanging outside the building, talking to local girls. Ramesh ignored their '*Kem cho, bhai?*' and carried on. It took courage to climb the narrow staircase of his building. He kept abusing the lift.

'*Saala*, the damn lift never works. These bloody Indians eat the maintenance money. I will show them tomorrow.' Hetal could hear the loud grumblings, as she had left their flat door open.

He toppled the steel water filter, kept in the left corner of the living room, as he barged in. The boiled and filtered water splashed all over. Hetal came out of the kitchen, went straight back in and reappeared with a mop. She bent down, exposing her neck and a few curls of grey hair. Ramesh looked at her, his wife appeared old, shabby and tired. She never fought, argued or asked for anything. She was a lifeless body who bore him children and kept his house. She had no spark of life left in her.

'*Ekdum* dull. *Suara nasha utar gaya saala*,' thought Ramesh. Hetal was thinking of boiling more water and that meant using the gas. Ramesh slurred, '*Aiy*, Hetal. Listen, wake me up tomorrow, early morning. And yes! I forgot to inform you that all of us are becoming Christians tomorrow. It is a good business deal. The church is very powerful and rich. Imagine, our children can then go to school for free and receive clothes, books and toys; and *saala*, they will speak English like the Americans, not waater, but warrer!'

Before Hetal could react, Ramesh was already snoring in his bed. Hetal took off his shoes and put a clean sheet on his body. He was reeking of alcohol. A trickle of saliva from his open mouth created a little wet patch on the beige bedspread, while sweat beads continued to appear like an angry rash on his forehead and neck. His breathing was irregular and heavy. He scratched his crotch, muttered something and laughed – a crazy muzzled laugh. Hetal had no tears left. Her ducts were dry, like the taps in her dilapidated house. She lived for her children. She had nowhere to go. Her father was long gone; the sisters married and living in different parts of Africa. Her brother ran the bookshop at Ahmedabad Railway station, which her father had started long back.

'Busy is the new word. They are all busy with their lives. And I am paying the price for some bad Karma from my previous life,' thought Hetal. She turned on the old AC, switched off the lights and tip toed to the living room, to inform the children. She had heard from her neighbours that two Sikh families from their neighbourhood had converted to Christianity. The two converted ladies visited other Indian families, holding copies of the Bible and tried to convert them. Most ladies in her building were not very happy with those two 'Hail Mary' chanting women.

Nine pairs of eyed stared at her with amazement, as she informed the children of their father's decision. What she didn't realise at that time was that the conversion would change their lives forever.

'*Mais Mamman nooooooo*,' screamed one.

The other sulked, '*Je la foot demain.*' Others looked on uninterested, fighting over the quilt, kicking, smacking and tugging at each other. One big hall in their old apartment roomed all the nine children. Three, three-tiered bunk beds occupied the three corners. Old smelly shoes, flip-flops, and some milk mugs were strewn around. Hetal looked pleadingly at her eldest son, Sameer, for rescue. She was spent and could feel all her life forces drain out of her delicate frame. She did not have the physical strength or emotional courage to deal with all their energies.

Her eldest son, all off thirteen and good-looking always came to her rescue, like one of those super heroes in the cartoons. It was a mother-son private joke. He promised never to abandon her, or to leave her alone at the time of crisis.

She loved how he would hold her wrinkled hand and kiss and say, 'Mamma stop doing the dishes, stop washing the clothes. Hire a domestic help. You need to go easy on yourself. I know you love the family, but *s'il vous plait*, don't be harsh on yourself.' Sam or Sameer had the advantage of good looks; deep dimples appeared on his cheeks when he grinned, and he had a thick mop of black hair and a tall lanky frame. He oozed charm, and always knew how to use that for his own benefit.

'*Ca va, Alors!*' He made a mock angry face at his siblings.

'Sleep now and we will think about it tomorrow. Shush... stop it, like, now, now! No arguments...*C'est finis...Mamman* has to sleep and we have an early day tomorrow.' He gave a tight hug to Hetal.

'*Khush reh mara dikra.*' All her troubles melted in that tight embrace.

'Stay happy and stay blessed,' she whispered. Hetal knew he would look after her, in her old age. He was that kind of boy who genuinely cared for everyone.

'Hope he doesn't follow his father's footsteps,' Hetal shuddered at the thought.

She tidied up the mess, before curling up on the old couch in the corner. It reeked of pee. Her little ones slept on this couch and often peed on it. Hetal couldn't sleep. She was playing with the end of her *dupatta* and thinking of what life could have been if she hadn't married Ramesh... did she have a choice... did she?

Her *Ba* had just walked in and announced, '*Tamara lagan nakki che.*'

'*Kem Ba?*' She had shouted. Her mother had shushed her.

'Other daughters have to be married too. The boy is from our neighbouring village in Gujarat. He lives in Ahmedabad and makes decent money,' her mother had said. She tried to recall the following events but couldn't.

'There is no point now. I am stuck with my bad Karma.' She sighed.

'Hetal *bhabhi*, dye you hair *ney* and wear tight, tight, *waistern draisses*. These Indian gents log only want one thing.' Hetal was often advised by other Indian ladies.

'*Na, na, manney nathhi gamey,*' was Hetal's usual response to all such suggestions of beautifying herself. She lay on her couch, wide-awake with random thoughts in her head. Hetal studied the cracks on the wall. She noticed the dull green curtains printed with a big, round face of former president Laurent Kabila. She received the fabric for free during the elections. She had stitched curtains with the leftover fabric, after making outfits for all her children. The face of 'Laurent Desire Kabila' was looking back at her too, expressionless, impassive and cold. It's strange that most of their clothes had faces of politicians and religious leaders staring out at the world. She had no direct connection with these people or their work, but she was grateful for the free fabric. Something told her that the current situation was about to change and she dozed off.

She was dreaming of their past life, way back when they lived in Goma, in 1997; when the rebel soldiers had marched into town, shooting indiscriminately.

'They spread across in files, high on weed, that's what the rumour is... shops have been looted, warehouses broken into and restaurants burnt,' her neighbour told her. Hetal was feeding her little one, she didn't remember which one though; while another baby kicked hard in her stomach, urging her to act and for once take some action in her life, and not be a mute spectator. "Boom, boom, boom," gunshots were rattling the windows. She ran with her children and her neighbour to hide in another room.

'The rebel forces are roaming the city like they own it. The soldiers look young. They must be under twenty. Their eyes are red and they burn with a sense of power. Power that comes with Kalashnikov. Whatever they loot is for them to keep. This is their real "salary". These "child soldiers" are trained in the interiors, by Mai Mai. It is believed that these children are "Pure"; and therefore, can perform black magic, and make potions or amulets. Their seniors make them conduct various magic rituals to make their bodies "bullet proof." and they this. They are the front liners. These soldiers are in demand in neighbouring Rwanda. With no education, healthcare and family support, they are easy recruit for the training camps,' her friendly neighbour informed her. She was a middle aged stout Congolese mamma who ran a little *alimentation* shop from the window of her house. Hetal got to witness their atrocities first hand. Children from their neighbourhood were reported missing.

'The Mai Mai and other military training centres are kidnapping them. There are rumours of rampant and indiscriminate rapes around town. The soldiers do not spare little girls or pregnant women. It is the worst face of humanity... The demons are parading, ruling and killing. The town looks hopeless dreary. The dead bodies lying unclaimed on the street, rotting and stinking. There is no one to claim or clear the bodies that are rotting on the streets. People are falling sick, diarrhoea and cholera are spreading like wild fire,' her neighbour said.

Ramesh had almost succumbed to cholera. His then boss refused to offer any financial help. She sold one of her gold bangles and took him to the local hospital, but it was worse than hell. The building was collapsing under the number of patients. The medical help had stopped coming from International aid agencies; and the few missionary doctors who were left, were over worked and sick themselves. She got him back home, almost carrying him on her slender shoulder, and nursed him back to health. All this, while also running the house. It was some power that had given her the strength at that time. This was the first time she sold off her gold bangles, all of 22 carat gold. Her *nani ma* had given them to her for her wedding.

Her grandmother had whispered in her ear, 'Give it to your own grandchildren.' A hint that she needed to reproduce soon. She had blushed. At that point, she couldn't imagine becoming a mother. How could she? She had seen so many Bollywood movies, and the wedding sequence was usually followed by the first night on a bed of flowers and later, what they called the Honeymoon. Singing, dancing, and romancing. It was difficult to let go of the precious bangles, but when she looked at the empty and hungry faces of her children and the condition of her husband, there was just no option. The kitchen had to run, the children and their father had to live.

Hetal walked up to the local *bijouterie*. Head bent, she tried to cover her face with her *dupatta*, the sun on the tar was too bright. Her cheap flip-flops could provide no relief to her sole that burnt, and the soul that squirmed. 'I must have done something really drastic in my previous life', a thought that never left her ever since she had gotten married.

'What was the bad karma and why doesn't the suffering ever end?' Hetal wondered. She silently accepted the money that was thrust in to her palm. She was too numb to argue or negotiate. The Senegalese shop owner offered her some beer, probably he felt guilty for paying a pittance for all that solid Indian gold. 'Ok *mamma, va, va. Je beaucoup de travais*,' he asked her to go.

'*Merci beaucoup pour l'argent.*' She was genuinely thankful. For a woman who had never ever stepped out of her house, to a woman who could sell off her precious family heirloom, the journey was immense. She didn't feel anything, thank god. Extreme emotions escaped her, and she did not need alcohol or weed for this. Hetal staggered back home. The plastic packets were heavy and she carried them possessed. Milk powder, rice, sugar, salt and some local medicine, and yes some peanuts for herself. Food for gold, at least the children will live to give her grandchildren. She smiled, *chalo* something to cheer about at last. But she did not want to 'evil eye' her happiness. God would take away her little happiness and leave her with tears.

She woke up the next morning, to her neighbours fighting next door. She gathered that there was a theft, and that 20 dollars were missing. Her Gujarati neighbour was yelling at her domestic help for stealing her money. The neighbour was abusing her and threatening to call the police. The noise subsided when the neighbour's teenage son woke up and admitted to sneaking out the money, for some fun with his friends.

'Trust Shehla to make a mountain out of a mole hill, *rai ka pahad* like we say,' Hetal thought to herself, as she walked into her kitchen. She brewed a strong cup of *masala chai* for herself with lots of milk, sugar, ginger and mint. She looked out of the kitchen window, while the muddy brown tea bubbled away. She added her spices while stirring it. The clock on the kitchen wall showed that there was still time for her to start her crazy spinning, to get the whole family ready.

It was early one morning in March, 2003. The neighbourhood had just begun stirring. The noise and bustling had not yet begun. The sun was mild. The apartment building housed mostly Indians, a few Congolese and two or three white expatriates. A Belgian businessman had constructed this thirteen-storey building in the early 20th century for his employees. The two tiny Schindler's elevators worked only if the guard on duty, on the top floor, heard the desperate banging from the other floors. The guard would run up to the floor above and release the rope, which pushed the elevator down. One had to bang on the door on the ground floor or scream out loud for the guard on duty, on the top, '*Papa, yaka... ascensuer.*'

'Get some exercise and walk up!' The guard would shout angrily, if woken up.

An Indian lady on the ground floor ran a little grocery shop. Another lady ran a beauty parlour, while most ladies sold Indian outfits and costume jewellery. This strategically located, tall and blackish-grey building right in the heart of *Marche de Commerce* was mini India. The stairs were splashed with the red spit of *paan*. The air hung heavy with the aroma of curry, korma and *samosa*. Some women in the building took orders for *dabeli*, *vada pao* and *puri bhaji*.

The blackish-grey building would come to life after 10:30 a.m. everyday. Women would come in to buy Indian groceries; men were constantly in and out to pick up *Pan Parag*, *gutkha* or *paan*. Drivers would come in to collect frozen and fresh fried, *samosas* and spring rolls. Then, would roll in the cars of rich *madames*, for facial and waxing. Hetal loved watching them from her kitchen window. They would delicately step out with their nice pedicured feet. Then with a look of disdain, they would handout a few francs to the guards, to allow their drivers to park their cars inside, while they got their facial done. Some local ladies who sold Indian vegetables, also sat in the parking lot and did brisk business.

'*Bhabhi*, *yaka*... come, come, fresh *kothmir*, curry *patta*, *gobhi*, *bhindi*, *marcha*. Good price.' They had picked up enough Hindi to sell their vegetables.

Hetal, was one of the few ladies in the building who did not run a business. She was a very good cook, and was often encouraged by the other ladies to start her own catering business. But, Hetal genuinely loved staying home to look after her kids.

Initially she was invited when the ladies in her building hosted kitty parties. She attended a few, but found them extremely boring. The ladies dressed according to themes, which included "going back to school," or "colourful" or "denim". They played bingo and bitched about people who were making money.

'*Tamey khabar che ney* ... psssss ... Oh his money comes from indulging in black magic ... So and so's husband has a black mistress ... Don't you know the trick?! If your business is registered under the name of a local woman, you don't have to pay tax! ... Bas *jalsa chey*, *bhabhi* ... You know some women know fetish and often do voodoo on men... no... giggled another one, mouthfull of *samosa*. 'These women are sexy. You understand no?! They are very good with sex. Tight in the front and tight at the back and tight breasts. What

else do our *aadmi* want?' '*Bhabhi,* You know the local girls
can do very good mouth sex!' '*Na na..* tell me you lying..
chhiii chiii.. hey *bhagwan,*' another would squeal. '*Arrey
bhabhi*, I'm saying truth only. These women in the nightclubs
go in the bathroom and take it in the mouth and do funny
things. They charge $20 I know of so many Indian men. 'Next
time we go to nightclub. O ho, you should see all the
shameless women there, no *laaj lihaaz* ...' Hetal hated such
conversations. They played bingo and a couple of other
games; fought over prizes; and cried fowl when the winner for
the best dressed was declared. But Hetal was never a party to
all this. Anyway, she wasn't invited anymore. She was too
simple. 'Sober', like the other ladies called her. She would
encounter these women, when the local ladies came selling
Indian vegetables in their building. The women would all
descend in to the parking lot, eyeing each other. Eyeing,
whose dressing sense has changed; who buys only potatoes.
And again the same stories.

'You know she is from my village near Porbandar. She
wore only cotton *chaniya choli* in the village and look at her
now, capri pants and a tight top.'

'*Bhabhi*, what you saying?! Nooo. Can't believe,' uttered
another.

'But see, her husband allowing *na*. Mine says "*Tu mari
biwi che… Ekdum tip top reh.*" *Maney* full jeans and tight
shirt. All cover, cover.' The local vegetable saleswomen had
learnt a smattering of Gujarati and would often joke, bargain
and talk to them in Gujarati.

After she finished her second cup of tea, the doorbell rang
and brought her out of her reverie. It was a young boy, maybe
thirteen or fourteen years old.

'Hail Mary!' he declared.

'You from Nigeria?' Hetal asked.

'Yes,' he answered, 'from Lagos.'

'I can understand from your good English,' she said. He was visibly pleased.

'Yes, not too many people here in Kinshasa can speak good English like us. Me, I no like French. Too difficult, man. But English, world language, you see.' He thrust a bag and a handwritten note from the church into her unsuspecting hand, and left. The note, written in a spidery handwriting, urged them to leave their house early and report on time. The church had organized a car for them. Hetal opened the big plastic 'Dubai Duty-free' bag to discover clothes. They were in various shades of white. So, this was it. It was for real. They were embracing a new God, and accepting a new way of life, and for once she felt good. She experienced a positive vibe. She could feel some unknown force taking control of her life and suddenly she there was a sense of peace. Finally, some method in the madness. The feeling was too good and she didn't want Ramesh to have a change of heart. This unexplained attraction towards a foreign faith. If her family heard of this, they would break all ties with her. No one in their entire village had ever thought of changing their faith. '*Jhala Ram bapa, Hetal gandi thayi gayi*,' is how her mother would wail, cry and beat her chest, when they heard of the conversion. But, she had reached a point of no return. Hetal made up her mind to truly love her new god, with or without her family's acceptance.

The pastor had sent the young boy to deliver the note asking the family to be on time for their conversion. It was a busy day for him and they shouldn't delay. The clothes were donated by the church to them, for the special day. The expat community had a large heart. They always donated nice and clean clothes to the orphanages and the church. While some were actually distributed among the needy, most were sold in the *marche*. This was also social service, the orphanage and church management reasoned. They had to keep their kitchen running.

The children were up. There was the usual fight over the use of the bathroom, towels, spilling of milk. Finally, they were bathed and changed into crisp clothes.

'It smells nice,' one screamed.

The other child yelled, 'Look there is a name printed inside my shirt, it says John, NY'.

'Mine is too big for me,' another cried. Hetal rounded them all together.

'Awwww... How good you look. Bright and clean for once.' She smiled.

Hetal oiled their hair and dexterously created a straight side parting, and neatly combed their hair, over howls and protests. All her kids hated this part of the morning ritual. They wanted cool hairdos like the local kids. They loved how they shaved little zigzag designs on their head. Thunderbolt, two straight line just above the ears. But, Hetal never allowed these luxuries. She chopped their hair herself.

'Why waste 10 dollars on a *coiffure dikro*? I can buy some vegetables for lunch,' she reasoned. All the screaming and shouting woke up Ramesh. He walked into the living room, rubbing his blood shot eyes and the kids started to exchange looks. A fly buzzed over his head, and he moved his head at various angles to avoid it. They did not dare laugh for the fear of getting thrashed. Ramesh's trousers had the fly open; the shirt was unbuttoned and crumpled; there was white dried saliva around the corner of his mouth. He looked as if he had had a rough night. 'Why you screaming?' he shouted at them. A sudden hush fell over the living room. The smiles and cries vanished. There was a strange silence – uncomfortable and unyielding.

'Hetal, there is wedding?' he slurred, still groggy.

'Why they dressed like a band party?' He wiped the saliva off with the back of his hand. The lone fly continued to buzz around him, as if angry for taking away something that was meant for it.

'The clothes are from the church, the pastor sent them this morning.'

'Oh, *teri toh*! That's how I woke up. *Saala* Pastor called early in the morning. *Allez allez toute le monde*. We have to be present on time and there is a taxi sent from the church.' Ramesh refused to wear the outfit sent from the church, instead he donned his own white safari suit and cheap aviators from the local market. He was happy to see his reflection in the rear view mirror. He applied cheap perfume under both his armpits, it left a circular stain.

'I'm looking cool, na?' He winked at his children. None of them responded except Sam, who high-fived him. Hetal squirmed at his bad breath. He was reeking of alcohol. Ramesh opened his mouth and sprayed some perfume inside.

'Oh oh... *Saala* it stings. But you never know,' he laughed. The children were squished in the car, they rolled their eyes, and shoved and pushed. One complained that his new shirt was itching him. Another one wanted to throw up.

The taxi driver kept cursing over the loud sermon that blared from the car stereo, "You will not covet other people's wife ... you will not steal... you will not make love to a monkey..." It went on and on. He hurled abuses at other drivers and pedestrians, and manipulated the car through the complicated streets of Avenue Commerce.

The family was received by the Pastor, at the big iron gate of the church. Two large palm fronds, intertwined to form an inverted U, were neatly balanced on the gate. A little sparkly and spidery handwriting declared '*Bienvenue*' on a white cardboard. The big 'Church of Redemption' building was still under construction. A list of people who had donated to the church was carved on a marble slab, at the gate. It listed all the rich Congolese musicians, politicians and businessmen. The path was lined with more palm fronds and dusty flowers. The compound wore a festive look. The locals, dressed in similar *paignes* or wax fabric were gathered in big numbers. The local women, flashy in their well-fitted fish-cut skirts and tights, laughed and joked.

'It is a feast for my eyes,' laughed Ramesh. 'Hetal, you must dress like this now.' He winked at his wife. Hetal was so busy taking in the atmosphere that she did not respond to his trademark frivolous comment.

The women in their bright *liputas* were busy pounding the *fufu* and preparing the *pondu* for the feast that would follow after the ceremony. The children stuck close to Hetal, they were bewildered and a little scared. None of them really understood the real implication of what was happening. They were too scared of their father's violent reaction and did not voice their concern. They looked around and exchanged looks with their siblings. Their mother appeared too dazed. She looked like a zombie possessed. A whiff of *poulet braise* and fresh *beigne* uplifted their spirit. The family was escorted to a make shift altar amidst claps, cheers and shouting in Lingala and French.

Their eight-year old son screamed, '*Pappa*, this looks like a hut and not like the church we watch in movies.'

Ramesh burst out laughing, 'Ha, ha, ha, *saala*... he is my real son! Pastor, look at my son, he is not impressed with your church.' And he backslapped the pastor who was visibly annoyed.

'Pastor, you eat too much money papa. Must share with church, no?' Ramesh lifted the thick gold chain from around the neck of the pastor, and drew him close.

'All church money glittering around your fat neck?' He laughed. 'I like your gold bracelet and watch. Let's do business together. I make you rich quick, quick. The pastor gently pushed him away and adjusted his gold rope around his fat neck. He was very upset with Ramesh.

'Ramesh, brother please be serious for once. It is a solemn event. The lord is waiting for you. Jesus Christ, the king of mankind will change your life.' The pastor gritted his teeth and walked ahead to start the ceremony.

Hetal had tears running down her cheeks, and she couldn't help sobbing into her *dupatta*. The children stood still, they didn't realise what was going on and Ramesh looked amused. He knew what he was doing. He was craving home cooked mutton *biryani* and spicy okra curry, a glass of chilled beer and some exciting time in bed.

'*Chalo*, let all this drama get over and I will treat myself to some English fun. New English God will provide some new type of English fun!' Ramesh looked amused.

'Pastor, nice women in the church, *Pappa*. Too much fun, you naughty old man eh? Sharing is caring. Don't forget papa!' Ramesh whispered, to the pastor. The pastor walked fast. He had never in his life experienced a man like Ramesh.

'Maybe the church will reform him,' he thought.

The altar was a solid black wenge table. Ramesh was quick to spot the timber, he had been in the business for long. The flowers and the palm leaves looked wilted, sad and beaten down by the hot sun.

The local community had gathered to witness this important ceremony. The Indian *mundeles* would embrace the divine path of Jesus Christ, the saviour. The church courtyard had been swept clean, but the avocado leaves kept falling over the palm leaves that had been used for decoration. People pulled out little packets of white *papier mouchoir* from their pockets, to wipe off the sweat. The priest conducted the ceremony with a lot of seriousness, while Ramesh kept looking at his watch. He had spotted a beautiful girl.

'She must be twenty. Look at her swinging her hips so provocatively, while singing and clapping with the choir,' he thought.

'Tight dress and big breasts, like ripe Indian mangoes. Just the way I like them, firm, not too hard and not too soft.' Ramesh smiled at his thoughts. Her skin was glistening against the sun. He noticed that she also looked his way, a couple of times.

'I will offer her a nice job. I know the trick to ensnare young girls. Offer them a job and they are quick to fall into the trap. Money boss! Money makes the world go round.' He was busy with his thoughts, while the pastor presided over the conversion ceremony.

Ramesh was getting edgy. He wanted to get over with the drama and receive the goodies. The holy water was sprinkled and the ceremony was completed. It was an awkward moment for the entire family. All eyes were on them, they did not know what to do. They were not a touchy-feely and hugging kind of a family. They exchanged glances and grunts.

The local parishioners gathered in the courtyard, sang their hearts out after the ceremony and very soon it was like a carnival. Time to dance and celebrate with Mutzig. They shook their bodies, gyrated their hips, and thrust their pelvis out to energetic beats. Kofi's "*Francs Congolais*" blared from the speakers. They were happy, content and enjoyed the rhythm. The children were sipping Djino, while Hetal had a few glasses of water to calm her nerves. She hugged the pastor and shook hands with the others. It felt right. She belonged here.

Dilpreet from her neighbourhood walked up to her. She now went by the name Esther, but the Indians continued to call her by her original name.

'Welcome to the community Hetal.' She held her hand and tucked a grey strand of hair behind her ear.

'You will find a lot of "our" people here and the locals are very supportive. My life changed for the better, ever since I joined the church. There is a purpose and meaning. We get together every Tuesday and Thursday afternoon, to read the bible and pray. Sunday everyone comes to the church. The church provides free bus service to all. I will introduce you to Shalu and Neelu, the two sisters, who are also part of our church. They couldn't make it today.' She hugged her. Hetal was still trembling, she wanted to breathe and breathe freely. The sun was getting hot, the music was loud and the dancing boisterous. She fainted right there in Esther's arms.

When Hetal opened her eyes, she was lying down on Esther's lap. And the community was shouting in Lingala and clapping. Their faces were excited and animated. She adjusted her clothes, and wiped her face as she got up. 'I'm sorry. I am fine. Sorry for this.'

'Don't worry sister. God is with you. It is a sign from god. You have been purified now. The devil has been taken out of your system. Hail Mary! Hail Mary!' they all yelled.

'You see *sistah*, you are purged now. The devil that was inside you has been pulled out. You are on the right path.'

Another said, 'She has come back from the dead just like the lord Jesus Christ!' They all clapped. This is the real church. Someone told her that she made the right decision by joining this church, and that there were so many others who practiced black magic in the name of the church.

'It works, they are for real,' declared Sophie, 'my teenage daughter was cured by them. The priest took out a piece of mutton from her stomach. Someone had done magic on my daughter because she was doing well in school. Now she is ok.' Others "tsked, tsked".

Mercy, a young girl also chimed in, 'My brother couldn't find a nice job as a gardener after his white *patron* left. They had given him an expensive bicycle and our neighbours became jealous. Someone did magic on him, and he couldn't find a job with white people. Then this pastor took out two big pieces of mutton from his mouth. And very soon he started working at two embassies.'

Philomina the old mamma, declared, 'The Nigerian priests are devils, they have sold their soul to the devil. There is no place for magic in Christianity. Please don't lose your path. Focus on the Bible.'

'Ok Pastor, *merci beaucoup*. I will go now. Hail Mary,' Ramesh giggled. The pastor was grateful that he had actually managed to stay calm during the ceremony. Ramesh went into the church office to finish all the paperwork. They were officially part of the church and were now entitled to all its benefits. He met some 'important people' of the parish, those who had just walked in.

'Life is set,' Ramesh thought, as he left the compound with the young girl he had been eyeing.

The feast continued in the courtyard. Hetal and children enjoyed a lovely meal of *fufu*, *pondu* and beef stew. They then went back to face the curious neighbours of their Avenue Commerce Building.

'*Bhabhi* you become Christian, how?' asked one.

Another one giggled and said '*Bhabhi*, you do black magic now?'

'I will tell you the truth,' Vimla screamed, from her balcony, while stringing green beans for dinner.

'It's that Dilpreet. Ever since she has become Christian, she goes to people's house carrying Bible. She says Hail Mary this and Hail Mary that. Trying to convert us, innocent Hindu people. I tell, stay away from her. I *toh* told her *saaf saaf*. You know I am so frank types. I said, look Preeto, you are welcome in my house for a cup of *masala chai, koki* even. But all this bible-shaible business, no way.' They all looked at her with admiration.

Muniba said, 'You know *bhabhi*, we have been told in our mosque that white people in groups are on a prowl these days. They travel in little vans, carrying imported gifts, trying to convert people to Christianity. We have been asked to stay away from them. You know our *patron?* He lives in Avenue Tshatschi, they came to his house. But *Madame?* Oh! She gave them good and also gave them a copy of the Quran in English. Read it, you guys, she blasted them.'

Hetal refused to comment. She smiled at them and herded the children up. 'I have to go. Dinner to cook.' And she walked up. She knew that she would be the hot topic of discussion during the ladies kitty, *sukhmani* path and Quran sessions.

Hetal was at peace with herself. She genuinely believed that her new god would guide her and protect her. The children had their glass of milk and went down to play, and Hetal sat down to read the Bible. Her hands shook, her body trembled and tears trickled down. This is it. She was on the right path. The doorbell rang.

'The children back so early?' she thought.

'Oh no, not another fight with the building bullies.' The kids these days fought over who has the latest Nintendo, PSP and other games. If their father went to the trade fair in China, they came back with fancy toys. This always started a fight in the parking lot. Hetal was preparing to scold her kids, but was surprised to see Dilpreet at the door. Dilpreet was carrying a home-baked chocolate cake that said '*felicitation*'. She kept it on the dining table.

'This is something small for the children, Hetal,' she said, and gave her a tight hug. She seemed genuinely happy.

'Hetal, welcome to our church. It's the wisest decision. You are on a path of salvation now. You know, I would have gone mad, but it's the church that saved me. When I was suffering, none of our people offered to help, but it was the church community that helped me cope.'

'I came here, long ago as a young bride from Punjab. My husband worked for a big Gujarati businessman, from Bombay. My husband was very clever, soon he started his own restaurant business. I also started working with him. Our business became big and we managed to send our children to the American School of Kinshasa. And then, he got cancer. We took many trips to South Africa for his treatment. Meanwhile, his two cousins ran the business. Then my husband passed away, I went through depression. One day when I went back to the restaurant, they had taken over the business. There was no place for me. From being the owner, to having nothing. I came crashing down. I abused them, screamed at them but they politely asked me to leave. The community elders, refused to intervene. They said it was a family matter, they couldn't do anything about it. How could they? These two men, my husband's cousins, had become very powerful importers with a lot of contact in the government. No one wanted to cross them. People forgot all the favours my husband had done for them. No one remembered our lavish parties, the gifts that we showered them with. They started avoiding me. I had to send my kids to

Dar es Salaam, to my brother, where they could get good education. Then, another Indian lady introduced me to the Church. *Bas, phir kya tha*... My life changed. The church helped me find a job in one of the nice boutiques in Grand Hotel that sells African artifacts. I work nine to five, from Monday to Saturday, and get together with other ladies to pray and heal. You know, prayers when said together, heal the world. I have no regrets, no ill feeling against anyone. The church is my family now,' Esther said.

Hetal sighed, 'I know Preeto. Thanks god, that Ramesh for once was wise enough. I know this will help me and the children. Let me get you some nice *masala chai* and you can tell me more about your group of praying ladies.' Hetal was happy.

The new religion helped Hetal cope with her miserable life. It changed her perspective, she no longer was a lost soul and she could feel the divine presence around her. She knew that her Lord was always there to protect, help and guide her. She now carried the bible and rosary wherever she went. The smooth brown leather on the cover of the book emanated some magic, because it gave her a real peace of mind. The rough gold embossed cross on the cover was her lucky talisman. It gave her special power. The church was her comfort zone. The children received good education in the church school. They would wear clean uniforms and rush to the school to learn and pray. She never failed to thank her husband for showing her the "true" path! 'O Lord! Dear Father! Be his shepherd... show him the path,' was her constant refrain on the rosary.

Hetal didn't know if her husband was dead or alive, in jail or travelling deep in the interiors. She maintained her sanity with the help of her prayer group. The women would gather every afternoon in someone's house to pray and discuss the bible. They greeted each other with "Hail Mary", "Peace be with you" or "Praise the Lord". Hetal encouraged some of her other Indian Hindu/Muslim friends to embrace Christianity, so that they could lead a better life. These women found comfort in the new religion that did not discriminate between rich and poor, and rallied around each other and offered support.

There was a strong rumour in the community that Hetal had something going on with the local pastor. He was often seen coming out of her house at odd hours. Hetal would go to the church often, which was now a concrete shiny building, and was seen talking to the pastor in private. She completely let herself go, her life now was dedicated to the service of the lord.

Manikchand, Makala and Money

Manikchand Seth was waiting to arrive. Each time Ramesh ripped open his Manikchand brand *gutkha* pouch and emptied the contents in his mouth, he felt a high, an unexplainable high; a rush of energy in his veins. Manikchand *gutkha*, a mix of betel nuts and other spices, was his constant companion and he was loyal to his brand. It was the old Gujarati man, the owner of 'Bombay *Masala*' – the Indian grocery store, who had started calling him Manikchand Seth. Ramesh always bought huge quantities of Manikchand *gutkha*. He placed an advance order for *Pan Parag* and Manikchand pouches. Soon the word spread and people started calling him Manikchand.

'I don't even remember to respond to my original name "Ramesh Patel". Anyway, it is too common. It could be Suresh, Ganesh or Jignesh, like so many of the Gujarati boys who work in the Marche in Commerce. They oil their hair and dexterously create a middle parting on their small heads. They wear their trousers just below the chest. It rests there all day, held tightly by a slim black belt. They run around from one shop to the other, or selling sundry items, and then sleep in a small paying guest accommodation with 8-9 other boys from their village,' Manikchand thought.

'They are all the same – pimply faced, unsure, cheap Indian labour exploited by family and family friends. The young man's family in the village received about 200 dollars monthly and everyone was happy. Ramesh enjoyed his new name, Manikchand Seth.

'*Saala*! Manikchand Seth. *Jalsa nam che.* Rich and powerful.' He enjoyed his new name. It offered some respite from the humiliation he suffered every day. It sounded rich and powerful.

'I work hard for these ruthless businessmen. What do I make in return? *Ghanta*! Peanuts! *Rien*! I also went to jail for them.'

Manikchand, *aka* Ramesh was restless. He wanted to do something dramatic to make fast money. He had heard of the legendary Haji Mastan in Bombay. The big boss who made plenty of money at the docks. He wanted to be the Haji Mastan of Kinshasa. The day had arrived and he was proud that he went to jail for his own doing. How proud and defiant he was, while going into jail.

'All great people go to jail. Mahatma Gandhi started his career in the jail!' he declared. Some people in the city laughed at him, some cursed him and some felt sorry for him. But Manikchand was glad to be in jail at that moment in time. It was destiny that drew him there, as if forces of nature conspired to pull him into that prison. It was in Makala prison that he met the 'right' people and made the 'right' contacts for himself. It was in this prison that he launched his own company.

That day changed his entire life. That day, the universe conspired, and the planets aligned to help him realise his dreams. He was at the right place at the right time and he was quick to grab the opportunities. He had only heard about the horrors of Makala prison, on the outskirts of Kinshasa. The hardcore war criminals, politicians and seasoned military men were locked up there on serious charges of crimes against the government, plotting a *coup d'état* or murders. He had been there once or twice to deliver money to prisoners from his bosses, but never experienced the deep horrific interiors of the infamous Makala prison. The money was always collected by an insider; outside of the prison. Makala prison was horrific. He had spent one night in a local police station, but that did not prepare him for this deplorable prison.

That fateful day, it was business as usual at the Kinshasa River port. Ramesh was chewing his *gutkha* and thinking of the curvy Bollywood babe Bipasha Basu.

'*Beedi jalile jigar sey piya, jigar ma badi aag hai... na gilaaf, na lihaaf, thandi hawa bhi khilaaf sasuri,*' sang Ramesh to Mansukh, a new arrival from Porbandar. Mansukh, eighteen years old, was slightly tanned from working at the Kinshasa port. He missed his family and food, but enjoyed his time at the port. It was a free society; unlike his village, the girls here were very bold and sexy. Right now, he was busy ogling at the local girls who walked around selling phone credits or just loitering.

'Manikchand *bhai*, if the *beedi* is struck from Bipasha's breasts, it will only catch fire, no?'said Mansukh. Ramesh slapped his thigh and laughed. '*Saala Mansukh, harami chokro che!*' He called out to Deven *bhai* who was constantly wiping his forehead with a striped nylon serviette, while talking to a new custom officer.

He spat the over-chewed red *gutkha* on the ground, cleared his throat and started singing in his throaty voice '*Beedi jalayli jigar se piya,*' he shoved his right hand under his green printed polyester shirt and massaged his chest. '*Toi, toi tu est mechant,*' laughed a young girl, who was selling Coke and Fanta from a small ice chest.

'Deven *bhai, aavi jao ney*, its lunch time. Let's enjoy some fresh and spicy *teekho-tekho dabeli*. I have asked for some extra *pili pili,*' Ramesh screamed out to Deven *bhai*, who was still wiping his sweat and struggling with his French, as the officer refused to speak Lingala. Deven *bhai* tilted his head and looked at Manikchand, he shook his head and looked at the sky. Manikchand walked towards them quickly. He held out his hand and said '*Mon frere, cava*? I know it's still Thursday, but for real men, its *Bon* weekend *deja*. Don't worry, I will give you something small.' He signalled to the girl selling coke and she ran towards him with her small ice-box.

'*Coca ezali? Pesa moko*,' he asked her to give him a chilled bottle. The officer took the bottle and finished it in one go.

'Aaah... *Ecoute ta soif*,' he laughed. The officer handed him his arrest warrant. Manikchand was accused of misleading and cheating the Port Authority of Kinshasa. He was immediately arrested at the port, and was convicted for cheating the customs department and not paying custom duties. It was a non-bailable offence, and he was immediately sent off to Makala prison.

Ramesh always took pride in his intelligence, he knew that he was good with "*jugaad*", and his "*jugaad*" was always mocked if he suggested his smart business ideas to his bosses.

'Boss, *bijness* is in my blood. I don't have any degree, but I have ideas and I have *jugaad*,' said Ramesh, often. He was glad that most outrageous business propositions were rejected, because he used them as his 'side businesses'. Later the same ideas were copied by others, to make money; but by that time it was too late, with too many players in the same market by then. There was a fire inside him, he could feel it in his heart. His hands itched for money and his mind was a workshop of innovative ideas. His physical body felt chained to the job, he was like a restless dog ready to loosen the leash and run away recklessly, be his own master, write his own destiny and create his own business empire.

'I am proud, hungry and shameless. I will make money,' he kept repeating to himself. His salary kept the family going, and the kitchen of his wife running. But he wanted more, more like the *patrons*; and he was restless for that one opportunity that would propel him in to the big league of 'Manikchand *Sarl*'.

'*L'argent*, money, *paisa…Saala* you need money to make money.' He laughed at his own joke.

The 'side income' was necessary to entertain and create contacts. He was always on top of new business trends, and kept his eyes and ears open. He was friends with most local business women who owned shacks near the Kinshasa river port, or who hung around CMK medical centre, or in *Centre Ville* – the heart of the market. They sold bright coloured fabrics called *Liputa*. The print on the fabrics had faces of political figures, cups and saucers, flowers etc. These fabrics were popular among both rich and poor. Though the rich often picked their fabric from Vilisco, while the middle class and poor bought it off the streets. Some women sold *brochette*, *poulet braise* or *fufu* and sauce on the street. He had good relations with the 'top mammas' who controlled other mammas on the street. He would often gift them Indian outfits – *saris*, *salwar kameez* or *Punjabis*.

'The mammas are my safe investments. I invest small in their business and they give back profit quick. The Congolese Mammas are honest, hardworking and smart. I enjoy my time laughing and eating with them. They often invite me for a meal of *fufu*, *pondu* and *liboke*. They also abuse me or call me *Mobulu* Manikchand, if I no buy them Guinness every Friday,' he would always tell his friends.

'The best place to gather gossip and business information is the local Indian *mithai* shop on Avenue Commerce.

Avenue Commerce is one long street with numerous electronics shops on both sides. The shop display often spills out on to the street. From televisions, to DVD players, music systems, pedestal fans, bicycles, generators, lamps, and cooking ranges; almost everything is on sale, from the pavement to the shop. There are various narrow streets that run parallel to Avenue Commerce and they specialize in different items. One street has shops that sell only curtains, bed sheets and fabrics. One street has small shops selling construction material. One street sells only car, bus and truck spare parts. The lanes are narrow, with open drains covered with stone slabs. Local hawkers sell undergarments, dried meat, dried caterpillar and grasshopper on the street. There is a constant stench of dried fish, generator fumes and sweat. There is hardly any place for vehicles. This is a haven for petty thieves and *shegues*, who pick pocket and demand money. The area is full of Congolese, Lebanese and Indian businessmen and workers,' Ramesh would tell the newcomers.

Ramesh loved the vibe of *Centre Ville*, it reeked with the smell of urine; there were betel nut and *paan* stains everywhere; the stereos in the shops played loud Bollywood music and the crime rate was high. It somehow reminded him of his own village, he felt at home here.

"Gokul, a little eatery at the end of Avenue Commerce was extremely popular. The owner's wife Mamta *bhabhi* was a look alike of Mamta Kulkarni, a Bollywood actress. She had the mouth of a truck driver and used the most colourful vocabulary. The young boys frequented 'Gokul', because *bhabhi ji* had very big breasts that popped out of her tight blouse and she was very careless with her *pallu*. She was the second wife of Lalu *bhai*, the shop owner. Lalu *bhai* sat in one corner chewing *gutkha* and reading old newspapers while his young wife ran the shop. She had the best *khakra, fafda, thepla, gulab jambo* and *dabeli* in town. She had a small TV fixed on top of the entrance door that constantly played B4U music, or sometimes a cricket match commentary. Manikchand liked the spicy food, sexy *bhabhi ji* and the busy restaurant. Gokul was extremely popular with the expat labour that worked in different shops. They gathered here to eat and exchange stories about their masters from Kinshasa, Matadi, Goma and Kisangani. Manikchand was always alert to pick up ingenious and innovative ideas on tax evasion, electricity supply and bills settlement.

'These are slaves. Motherfuckers, they will never grow in their lives. Their mentality is subservient. They are happy working with someone from 8 a.m. to 5 p.m. in the shops and later in their houses.' He never felt sorry for them and their plight, because they could only be slaves. He would listen to the latest gossip and enjoy his *samosa*, *vada pao* and *chai*. 'Leave the labour class to go back to back breaking work,' he laughed.

Manikchand was on an accelerated program, he wanted to be rich and he wanted to be rich "now, now". He had spent many years in Africa and time was running out. He identified that hunger for quick money in the new manager of the local Chinese Restaurant and Supermarket. '*Patron Chinoise*', as he was called, was quick and clever. He picked up Lingala and French like a native, and most importantly convinced his boss to move to Brazzaville and start a new business, while he ran the show in Kinshasa. There were a lot of stories in circulation about him on Avenue Commerce. Some said, he married a beautiful rich Congolese and together they owned few small mobile and mobile accessories kiosks. Others argued that he had greater plans; he was actually planning to marry the owner's daughter and be part of the family. Manikchand kept a close watch on him. The young Chinese manager was often seen driving with the old man's wife to the golf course, and sometimes he walked with his daughter by the Congo River after closing the shop. Both, mother and daughter seemed to enjoy his company and they laughed at what he said. The owner was busy setting up a new business in Brazzaville, for he trusted his new manager with his business, wife and daughter. '*Patron Chinoise*' had made himself indispensable to the owner in every way. The profits soared after he took over the running of the day-to-day business. He sacked a few old Chinese staff who cursed and abused him, but quickly opened their own little restaurant and shop. The Old Chinese owner was very happy. Manikchand was deeply impressed by '*Patron Chinoise.*'

Manikchand knew that the Chinese Manager and he were meant to be. He called up the restaurant "*Le Orient Rouge*" and reserved "*Salle prive*" for himself. The small room inside the restaurant was the premium room, with a table of twelve meant for intimate gatherings or business meetings. The *Salle prive* came at a premium of $500. It was also a status symbol to dine there, away from the prying eyes of everyone. Manikchand walked in at 9 p.m. He was dressed in a grey safari suit, a wornout brown leather pouch dangling from his wrist. He stared into his new phone while chewing on his *gutkha*. He waited at the foyer with other rich expats to get into the lift. He was claustrophobic and this lift was notorious for breaking down in the middle of a ride. The restaurant was on the 8th floor of a rickety old Belgian building. The Schindell's lift was probably never serviced after the original Belgian inhabitants left. Now, mainly offices and some UN employees occupied the building. *Le Orient Rouge* served the best Chinese food in town, and was very popular among the expats and local elite.

He entered the lift with two other couples. He was nervous in the closed space, and hated the intense perfume that one of them was wearing. He tried to focus on their cleavage, but both were almost flat. He felt sorry for their men.

'*Bicharo*, no meat on their women. No *mazza, masti* for them,' he thought and chuckled. The women found him staring at their breasts, and they rolled their eyes and walked out immediately after the lift stopped on the 8th floor. He left after them and walked in proudly, as the Chinese doorman opened the door for him.

'*Bon soir*! *Bienvenue*,' the guard bowed.

Manikchand thrust a $5 bill in his hand and murmured, '*Bonsoir.*' The guard looked at the note and smiled.

'*Bonsoir,*' he greeted him loudly, and escorted him to the private dining room. Manikchand stared at the crowd while walking in.

'Let the motherfuckers, bloody expats see that I dine here too.' He felt a seething anger within him. He had to make money somehow. 'No money, no power and no respect'.

His thoughts were interrupted by a Chinese manager, 'You wait for your people or you order now?'

'I wait for your *Grande Patron*, *appelez lui*.' In walked the famous manager, '*Patron Chinoise*', dressed in a white and pink striped cotton shirt and white trousers. His hair slicked back with gel, a twinkle in his eye.

'Good looking in Chinese way,' thought Manikchand, as he got up to shake hands with him.

'*Assez vous monsieur*,' Manikchand asked him to sit next to him.

'*Pesa Band noir, double, pappa kende, kende,*' he asked the waiter to leave them alone. They hit it off instantly and spoke like old friends. When they finished dinner at 2:30 a.m., they back slapped, high fived and collided their heads three times like the local Congolese. They sealed the deal and were business partners. No documents signed and no *maitre* as witness. Manikchand invited him to *Wild Nights*, a nightclub in *Bon Marche*, but he refused as he had work the next day.

Both knew that they had hit a jackpot with Manikchand's idea, and hoped that it would work.

Ramesh had a keen eye, he realised that there was a huge demand for footwear, but supply was limited and very expensive. He ordered a container full of plastic shoes, sandals and fake crocs from China. His first container arrived on time and without any damage. He was excited, his first big venture. He and the Chinese manager had a lot riding on it. It was their own money and their independent business. When they opened the container, there were only left shoe of a pair.

'Chief, *venez voir*,' he called out, to the big burly custom inspector Matondo. Inspector Matondo laughed when he looked at content of the container. '*Allez... laisse passe.*' He waivered the custom duties and left. He sat on the port complaining to the port authority, about how he had been duped by the Chinese and had lost all his money. He had ordered a container full of shoes, sandals and slippers of different sizes; and all he received was half the pair. The right shoe from the pair was missing. The port authority let him off without paying the custom duty.

He off-loaded the container, then sold all the shoes just outside the Congo river port with the promise to provide the right side, after two weeks. And he actually did. Another container arrived with the right side of the same pair. Another customs officer, who felt sorry for this Indian man struggling to set up a new business, let him off.

The buyers were extremely happy with their brand new pair of plastic sandals at such a cheap rate. Word got around the market and local customers were booking their pairs of shoes in advance. Some local mammas who sold undergarments and shoes in baskets, sought Ramesh and became his dealers; and then onwards he didn't have to physically sell the shoes. The tough Congolese mammas handled the sales for him. This went on for a long time, his Congolese mammas asked for fancy gloves, clothes and plastic dinner sets. This business model worked perfectly well. Everyone got their share from the trade.

Then one day the Customs department had a major shuffle. New officials took charge and the old ones were shunted out. The Customs department had a new head, who wanted to create a name for himself among the importers. No one among the business circles knew him, and he refused to be pacified with small sums of money.

When the next container arrived, Ramesh went to the port to release it.

'*Eh toi*, Ramesh... *Toi, tu est compliquez.*' The new inspector wanted more money out of Manikchand. By the time the third and the fourth container arrived, the inspector was out to get him. Manikchand was arrested at the Congo River Port and sent to Makala. He spent fifteen days there, till his Chinese partner bailed him out.

Makala Prison

Makala was not meant for the fainthearted. Situated outside the city limits, Makala is known as the worst prison in Africa and it lives up to its reputation. Crumbling walls, dark cells and no ventilation made it difficult to breathe. The strong stench of urine, vomit and cannabis added to the queasy feeling. Manikchand had a strong premonition that his life was about to change.

'What an experience in jail. *Ara ara ra. Jhalaram Bapa*! I am glad I met these people in prison who changed my life.' He was grateful for the prison experience all his life. He was locked up in the same cell as a powerful old Juju man; a *metisse* businessman; an old disgruntled politician; and a warlord who traded guns, diamonds, cobalt, salt and drugs.

'Such a royal gathering of people!' thought Manikchand. 'Boss, *uparwala ustaad*, he has great plans for me. Why was I put in the same cell as all these powerful people? *A ra ra... Su vaat che*!'

The old Juju, was a mini celebrity in the region and commanded a lot of respect among all the inmates. He was always busy receiving high profile visitors after midnight. The list included top musicians, businessmen and politicians. He was put behind bars because a powerful church pastor filed a criminal case against him. The pastor, when he had just started off, sought the Juju's help with growing and spreading his church. The pastor experienced overnight success and he continued to pay the Juju. The pastor claimed that he had loaned $20,000 to the Juju, and that he had refused to return it. The Juju denied that he had ever borrowed the money, and said that he had no means to pay it back. The jail authorities treated him with a lot of deference, and the inmates always greeted him with respect.

One night was exceptional in the dark Makala prison. There was a flurry of activity, a lot of hustle and movement. And in walked Roger Kinky, the most famous musician of Congo. His guards and flunkies waited outside, while he hugged the old Juju inside the cell and wept. Ramesh was in a corner, straining his sharp ears to overhear their hushed conversation in Lingala. It turned out that the musician was deeply in love with his *patron's* wife. *Madame Patron* and the musician were madly in love, but both did not have the courage to upset the super-rich *patron*. Roger Kinky sought the Juju's help to replace his *Patron's* intense love for his wife with hatred. So that, the *Patron* continues to support Roger's music and does not seek revenge. Otherwise Roger will be forced to steal the *Patrons* wife. The Juju said, he will try his best. The Patron was also the Juju's ardent follower, and never took an important decision without consulting the Juju. Many politicians and powerful men too, visited the Juju at night. One warlord arrived with his new Commander-in-chief and wanted special blessings. *Madame* Obiya, an important minister wanted to get rid of her greedy stepson, and her daughter to fall out of love with a local not-so-rich businessmen. The old Juju heard each one patiently. The rich and the mighty did not seem to mind the dirt and the filth around the cell. They came to him looking for a solution to their problems. He was the king of the night, his powers were strongest when the forces of darkness were active. No one wanted to acknowledge him during the day.

The Juju man's nights were spent meeting powerful people, making sacrifices of specially picked roosters, slaughtering animals, making amulets or contacting the ancestors.

'I am in touch with the powers of the old forest. The ancestors are happy with my work. They collaborate with me. I start my séance by invoking the spirit of the ancestors. Modern Africans have denounced their own religion and their ancestors so the ancestors have also abandoned them. But, the old forest and spirit of their forefathers, holds the key to all their solutions. People should ask for forgiveness, and worship their ancestors and the sprits in special masks,' he confided in Manikchand.

The Juju spent his day eating and sleeping because his nights were alive and active. He was listless and irritable during the day. He lay on a blue and green plastic mat, a luxury in the prison. A big plastic bag held his prized possessions. This bag was treated with utmost reverence. It was from here that he doled out amulets, herbs and other cures. He owned two pairs of black ankle-length *boubou*. Manikchand bonded well with the old Juju. He shared his food and bitter cola nuts with him. The other powerful inmates also took a strong liking to Manikchand. He made them laugh with his crass jokes; and entertained them with his anecdotes from the River Port, customs officials and the *gendarmes*. They were quick to notice Manikchand's sharp brain, smart business acumen and his go-getter attitude. Manikchand's close contact with the prison guard kept a steady supply of chilled Guinness beer, *gouba* (peanuts) and *Endomie* instant noodles.

Manikchand learned from the prison guards that the warlord was extremely powerful in Eastern Congo, Rwanda and Burundi. He controlled the businesses and his private army continued to rule in the interiors. Manikchand, had impressed the warlord and he resolved to do business with his new Indian '*Frere*'. The *metisse* businessman, scion of an old rich Belgian-Congolese family, was back in Congo from Burundi to claim what was rightfully his. He owned a lot of property all over Congo, and ran a huge transport business in

Burundi and Congo. Each one gradually realised that they needed each other to facilitate the change they wanted to see in the country. The time was just right to launch their secret mission. Ramesh was in the right cell, with the right company, and at the right time. The Universe had truly conspired. The men in prison agreed to create an alliance that would change the economy and politics of the country. They were itching to unleash their secret plan.

The trio hadn't slept a wink, as they discussed their top-secret business project. The old Juju was sitting quietly in a corner. He rolled his joint with great precision, took his first drag and closed his eyes. He sat still, smoking, but was attentively listening to their conversation. Hurried phone calls were made to many local and International contacts. Things automatically fell into place. They were totally charged up, and couldn't wait to walk out of prison and get cracking.

It was 6 a.m. and the inmates were shouting to use the toilet and get some clean drinking water. The old Juju got up from the corner and walked slowly towards his mat.

'*Bonjour, Pappa* Juju,' greeted Manikchand. The old Juju ignored him and lay down on his mat.

'Tonight, the spirits of the ancestors will roam the city. You offer wine and whisky to appease them. They will bless your partnership. Arrange for the sacrifice, such celestial nights occur once in thirteen years. You are lucky,' the old Juju declared in his raspy voice, and fell into a deep sleep. They could hear him snore. Their day was spent organizing the special offerings for the sacrifice, along with planning their future joint venture.

It was past midnight and the ceremony had just begun with traditional rituals. The old Juju chanted, while the goat provided by the jail warden, bleated. With a strong movement of the machete, he killed the goat. Blood splattered all over. The old Juju, danced around the dead goat and smeared blood on their faces. Ramesh recoiled when the Juju leaned in to anoint him with blood.

'*Jamais*. Never do that. Never reject voodoo blessings. It make you rich and gives you the special powers. If you turn away, it will move away from you.' The old man presided over this solemn ceremony. He signalled them to hold hands. They formed a circle and held hands around the corpse of the goat, and sealed the final business deal. The old Juju man tied a sacred amulet around their necks and blessed them. In the darkness of the night, a little candle flickered in the small, smelly prison cell. The Juju man danced around the candle. He was screaming, shouting and crying. No one dared to move. They stood still, trying to focus on the future that awaited them. The Juju man collapsed on the cement floor. A big rat ran over him. His eyes were upturned, and the index finger of his left hand pointed towards the small window in the cell. Did something move? No one was sure. They stood there transfixed. Manikchand couldn't bear the stench of the blood and he threw up right there. The night guard entered their cell at that moment, swearing at them. 'What is this? Which of you is making the cell dirty?' He was obviously not from Congo, as he spoke English. The night guard froze at the sight of sacrifice. He politely requested the inmates to spend the night in another cell. The next day, they were released.

No one knew of their deal, but their success was unprecedented after they exited from the prison. Manikchand had joined the brotherhood and formed a secret pact with the old politician, the warlord and the businessman. An important event was about to happen. Manikchand walked out of Makala prison knowing fully well that he would make money and history. He didn't care much about history though, but he loved money.

Kalashnikov and Kinhasa

The Democratic Republic of Congo was stagnant. The burgeoning population was waiting for a messiah and a positive change. These days, the locals often discussed how they ate plenty of fish with their *fufu*, during President Mobutu's time. There was a sense of nostalgia, a sense of pride for former Zaire. They craved for President Mobutu and the good times. The current president, Joseph Kabila took over from his father, Laurent Desire Kabila. The young President Kabila continued to be in power. The economy was sluggish, unemployment was at an all-time high, and the currency had hit rock bottom against the dollar. The government minted small Francs, but the business still happened in dollars. Inflation had hit everyone, salaries were paltry and the cost of living was sky-rocketing. There were no jobs. Majority of the population fled the villages to seek a life in the city. Kinshasa was bursting at its seams. There was hardly any electricity and portable water, in the interior of the city. Medical facilities were non-existent, and education was beyond the reach of the locals. However, the rich locals and expats continued to live in a bubble, and shop at exorbitant super markets like City Market or Alimentation Express, where a carton of milk cost $10. The *shegues* or street urchins ruled the streets. They banged on cars till they were paid a few dollars. The police force was dissatisfied with their allowance. They constantly demanded '*Pour Boire*', or a tip at every crossing. The ministers were constantly changed to appease everyone in the ruling party. General elections were postponed twice. Political ambition was brewing among the old politicians, who had fallen out of favour. Everyone complained about the corrupt system. 'No bribe, no work,' was the order of the day.

A powerful cartel of warlords wanted complete control of the mines in Eastern Congo. Their leader was out of prison, arranging more funds for their private army. The old politician, wanted to come back to power and change the fate of the country. The *metisse* businessman wanted exclusive contracts to build the rail lines, roads, and supply trucks and other machinery. He was outraged to see his country being exploited by the Chinese. The Chinese grabbed all the major contracts, while the locals didn't even get crumbs. The secret alliance of the prison inmates kicked off with the blessings of the old Juju man. They fitted in perfectly, like a perfect jigsaw puzzle. Together, they minted money and achieved the unimaginable.

Manikchand played a small part in the big scheme of things. It was alleged that he had become a kingpin in smuggling arms, diamonds and gold from the interiors into the city. There was a lot of activity on the small river ports; containers full of arms and ammunition were being brought into the city. No one could fathom the scale of the big plan. The plan that shook the entire country in March, 2006.

Manikchand couldn't sleep at night. He was working around the clock, receiving truckloads of arms, currency and combat gear. He had a whiff of what his partners had been planning, but nothing had prepared him for what happened on that fateful day.

He had never seen so many guns come into Kinshasa. He was personally supervising the delivery of arms and cartridges, hand grenades and mobile phones. Trucks and boats were busier than ever. It had to be done quietly, in a guarded manner. No one was a friend these days. Manikchand personally supervised every big offload and delivery. Soldiers were secretly taking position in and around Kinshasa. There was tension. Something very big was about to occur.

Manikchand was making money like never before. He felt fearless and was like a man possessed, for once he was making money for himself. These big Congolese men respected him for his work and worth. Unlike his Indian bosses, they addressed him with respect, calling him '*Mon frere*'. They gave him his share, in cash, always on time. It was a dangerous mission, it gave him a thrill. Money never failed to excite him. He wanted an encore. Manikchand's partners had other big partners too, who were planning to overthrow the current government, and take complete control of the country.

MARCH, 2006

It was a balmy morning. The boulevard was jam-packed. An old Volkswagen had broken down causing a massive jam. The bylanes towards the golf course were also jammed. The MONUC soldiers stationed next to the UN office looked bored. They stood next to their white tanks. Some MONUC soldiers' patrolled in their white Land cruiser painted with a big black UN sign. *Avenue de Commerce* was buzzing with the usual activities. The Golf course had its regulars playing golf and tennis. *Cercle Elaise* swimming pool was full of expats, swimming and tanning themselves. The gym next to the pool was bustling, with people sweating on different machines. The coffee shop at Grand Hotel was packed to capacity. Businessmen, traders and middle-men were all at work. There was nothing different about today.

The first shot was fired at around 10 a.m. near the Spanish Embassy, just behind *Avenue de la Justice*. The hand grenade fell right on the embassy oil reserve, and soon the embassy ground was ablaze. Another grenade fell on the *Jamatkhana*, the Ismaili Mosque on the boulevard. The tin roof of the

Jamatkhana courtyard ripped open. There was pandemonium. The rebels had moved into the city firing indiscriminately, shattering window panes, blowing up roofs, and killing anyone that came in their way. A big group of rebel soldiers were firing non-stop at the window of the American Embassy. The bulletproof glass refused to shatter, and this confused and enraged them further. The attempted *coup d'état* was for real and no one had anticipated it. The intelligence at different embassies was completely clueless. It was a rebellion led by Vice President Jean Pierre Bemba. The rebels had taken control of the local TV station and Radio Okapi. The shopkeepers hurriedly pulled down their shutters. It was raining bullets in Kinshasa city.

People were screaming for help and shelter. Most embassies rushed their staff into their safe rooms. The diplomats, locked up in their safe rooms, were trying to assess the situation, and contact MONUC for help. Students were stuck on campus at the American School of Kinshasa. There was no way parents could drive up to the school, to pick up their children. All they could do was pray for their safety. Thankfully, mobile phones were still working, so they could keep in touch. People were stuck in their offices while the city burnt. The only source of information was CNN, that too only in areas that had power. The UN forces rolled in their mighty tanks, trying to rescue those who were stuck in dangerous areas. Mothers with small children hiding between walls of their houses, children stuck in different schools and some important dignitaries caught off guard in meetings.

Manikchand was working from his new 10th floor office on the boulevard. It was an old high-rise apartment building. He and his staff were crouching on the floor in the store room. Two stray bullets fell next to their feet. He could feel sweat drops trickling down his armpits. His mouth was dry and his heart was beating faster than the gunshots. His staff were shaking and crying. His accountant, Mamma Rosali was on her knees praying and asking for forgiveness. Three bullets rammed straight into the cupboards. There were glass splinters everywhere.

'Lay down on the ground,' he instructed. Everyone found safe positions between walls. Manikchand squeezed himself under the slab in the small pantry. This spot was safest in his office. His phone was beeping, it was a missed call from Hetal. He called back instantly, for once.

'Hetal, *cava?* Where are you?'

Hetal was sobbing, 'I managed to get three kids from the school. I am near the Mercedes roundabout, and the driver is shaking and can't even drive straight. I am crouching down in the car with the kids. The bullets are flying all over our heads. There are dead bodies everywhere.' She was praying and sobbing.

'Hetal, rush to Ghazala *bhabhi's* house in *Socimat.* Don't move towards *Avenue de la Justice* or the boulevard. Go now. *Allez rapide,*' he urged.

Window panes were shattering and the door rattled. Suddenly there was a heart-wrenching wail next door. Manikchand carefully crawled out on all fours, and opened the main door of his office to check outside. His Chinese neighbour lay dead right in front of him. Two bullets had gone straight through his heart. There was blood everywhere. The Chinese office assistant was trembling and crying.

'How?' Manikchand managed to ask the Chinese lady.

'He go out for small smoke and to click pictures.' Another bullet landed right next to her. She fell on the floor and Manikchand shut the door of his office, and crawled right back in to the pantry. Manikchand's phone was ringing non-stop. It was Hetal again.

'Yes Hetal. You safe?' He was genuinely worried for her and the kids.

'I am at Ghazala *bhabhi's* house with the three small kids, but the rest are still stuck in school. I spoke to their teacher, and she assured me that they are fine and safe on campus,' she said.

'Hetal, I can hear gunshots. Why are you not inside the house? Go in now, now.' Hetal did not want to tell him what had happened at Ghazala *bhabhi's* house. It was a woman's thing. She would keep it in her heart like many other things. His phone rang again. It was his Indian Manager.

'Boss, we are on the 8th floor of the apartment building at Centre Medical Kinshasa, the high-rise opposite the Kinshasa port. Its death and destruction everywhere. The windows are all broken. One bullet landed on the bed and split it into two. The neighbours are saying that the soldiers have entered the building. Boss they are looting and raping women. They are already on the third floor, and soon they will get us on the eighth floor. Save us, boss,' he was crying.

'Don't believe in rumours. Be strong. I am sending a big army man to get you out.' His phone had a call waiting; it was his Lebanese partner in his water business, on the line.

'*Grande patron*, the soldiers are banging on our factory door. I have pulled the shutters down and closed the plant. Bullets are raining in our backyard. Our young Lebanese boys are terrified and hiding in the factory. But don't worry, I am in control.'

'*Merci*, my brother. I know you are strong. Nothing will happen. I am there.' He disconnected. He respected the Lebanese; they were smart, strong and practical businessmen.

The rebels had taken over the city and it was complete mayhem and terror for three days. His phone rang again and it brought a smile to his face, it was Lakha *bhai*, his old boss.

'Ramesh, where are you? I need help now,' he ordered.

'It's a *coup d'état*, Lakha *bhai*. Anything can happen. Stay safe.'

'Wait don't disconnect, Ramesh,' Lakha *bhai* pleaded.

'Yes, say fast, I am busy Lakha *bhai*,' Manikchand had had his revenge. Finally, his bastard ex-boss was pleading in front of him.

'My milk powder warehouse is completely looted. The container had just arrived, and the entire stock of milk powder has been looted by the soldiers. All that is left is hundreds of pairs of slippers. The bastards have carried even the twenty-five kilo sacks. Do something fast.'

'You have insurance *na*? *Vanda nathi* boss. You will get your claims. You should worry about your other hanky panky business, Lakha *bhai*. Times are changing.' He disconnected and looked up at the sky. Another bomb exploded on the boulevard. He had arrived. The gods were declaring it to the world.

'Watch out world for Seth Manikchand,' he thought.

Manikchand and his staff survived on water, milk powder and coffee for three days. He managed to arrange for some baguette and mayonnaise for his staff stuck in other places. His accountant, Mama Rosalie, was diabetic and couldn't get her medicine. She had to be rushed to the hospital urgently.

Vice President Jean Pierre Bemba, the leader of the rebellion was finally flown out of Kinshasa. The soldiers ran out of resources, and the leadership and the government was back in control, once again. The city was inching back to normalcy. The locals needed money to survive, they immediately reported back to work. Manikchand was extremely busy becoming Manikchand Seth, The Boss. His life was dramatically changing.

Hetal was the same. Her life revolved around the church and her children. Manikchand lived in a villa on *Avenue de Justice*, and moved his family to a posh apartment on the Boulevard. She was sipping her *masala chai* and thought of what she had witnessed and heard, on that fateful day at Ghazala *bhabhi's* house.

11:00 a.m., Kinshasa, 2006. Attempted *coup d'état* by the private army of Jean Pierre Bemba. Hetal reached Ghazala's house. The main door was open and she quietly went in. Her three little kids were tired, she gently put them on the bed in Ghazala's guest bedroom. She sat on the sofa and took out her Bible. She didn't want to disturb Ghazala.

Ghazala was sleeping peacefully in her small house on the outskirts of *Socimat*, Kinshasa. The air conditioner whizzed, lulling her to a gentle sleep. The room was icy cold; she pulled her duvet close to her and hugged the pillow. Aaah the luxury of late morning sleep. Husband at work, children in school and she had no catering orders for today, so she let her cook go. It was so beautiful. She was dreaming of the warm beaches of Mombasa, the hot *chai* and *chana bateta*... The idle gossip with the extended family outside her mother's shop. The familiar smell of the ocean... The call for prayers... The tangy taste of dried mangoes, and how she loved to nibble on them with a dash of red chilli and rock salt. As she swirled her pink tongue around her mouth, she felt the dryness, and was jolted out of her delicious reverie.

Bang, bang bang... gun shots... Her first instinct was to feel the money that she always tied around her *shalwar*. Her dollars were safe. Years of living in turbulent conflict zones in Africa had taught her to keep money in a secret pocket, stitched on the band of her *shalwar*; just like her mother and grandmother had done. She quickly adjusted her *hijaab* and rushed to the window to take a peek.

It was 12:10 p.m. The neighbourhood appeared deserted... The rebel soldiers were everywhere... firing randomly, shattering windows, bringing down roofs and trying to pillage the shops.

'*Ya khuda, raham.*' Her hands went up in prayer. She read a quick little prayer and tried calling her husband on his mobile. He owned a few electronic shops in the heart of the commercial district of Kinshasa. But on a day like this, the network was jammed and the call wouldn't go through. She knew he would be safe somewhere. Though he was relatively new to Africa having spent only 8 years to her lifetime, in Africa. He had adapted quickly to the ways of commerce here; and he rarely spoke about his life in the tiny hamlet of Gujarat.

'He is a survivor, he will find his way!' she thought. Her heart was in her mouth, her three precious children were in school.

'Not again... not another *coup d'état,*' Ghazala prayed. She had seen her father suffer – from being the richest businessman in Kampala, reduced to a shop assistant in his cousin's shop in Mombasa; and then starting all over again with two grocery stores.

She chided herself, 'Ghazala control yourself! This is no time for an emotional flashback.' She could do that some other time at leisure, when she would savour each and every reel of her past life, smiling a little, wiping a tear drop; and then feeling the heat rising around her cheeks, with the tender memories of the flush of first romance on the pristine beaches of Mombasa. 'Hold them... the flooding thoughts, Ghazala.'

Hetal was busy reading the Bible. She wanted to finish reading the New Testament before coming out of the guest bedroom to greet Ghazala.

'She will understand,' thought Hetal.

Ghazala jutted out her chin, she was in control now, after all, and she had seen three life changing pillages. A small frown appeared on her forehead, as she dialled the number of the school reception. 'Please God,' she pleaded with the almighty, 'let the call go through.' She tapped nervously on the window pane, while she took a quick look at the worsening situation outside.

As if on cue the school receptionist answered her call, 'Don't worry Mrs. Ramji, the children are safe in school and we are here to look after them.'

'*Shukar*,' she muttered. The American School campus would be the safest place for her children. She made a mental note to do a *sadka*, the minute the city came to normalcy.

Hetal was shocked when she saw Ghazala walk up to the kitchen and pour herself some stiff Vodka. Ghazala needed to survive this moment. She opened the door of the refrigerator, and caressed the ice cubes. How she loved and welcomed the little shiver that went down her body. The star-shaped cubes tinkled into her Vodka and she gulped her drink down, while slowly adjusting an old family picture stuck on the fridge by a cheap, made-in-china, fruit magnet. She stared at her old father, her beautiful mother, and her ruthless, aging grandmother.

'Ohhh... the way my mother suffered under the old witch.' Ghazala remembered. The battle continued, because her *dadi* still hadn't forgiven her mother for delivering two girls and no boy.

'Who will carry forward the name of our illustrious family?' The old witch would complain, to every willing ear, 'No *chokro*,' and she would let out a wail, '*yaa khudaaa.*'

'Illustrious?! My foot!' thought Ghazala. Wasn't her grandfather the biggest womanizer? He had slept with so many African women and fathered all those half-caste children. Her father, being the eldest and 'rich' at one point, had the responsibility of settling them, taking them to the mosque (lest they become *kafirs*), and getting them married.

She gulped the Vodka down. 'It will help me get through... this time will pass. The country has suffered so much already it just cannot afford another disaster. The city has to calm down, after all there is a huge UN presence here. But those UN *haramis* don't do anything apart from sleeping with the local girls. They zip around in their white Land Cruisers, predator like, on the streets looking for easy victims. They provide business to the nightclubs' local proprietors, couple of them getting together to rent apartments and increasing the local house rents,' thought Ghazala.

She then remembered to switch on the TV. The local station was already captured by the rebels and there was no broadcast. Her phone rang breaking the eerie silence of her house. It was her friend, Shahida. A teacher in a local school, Shahida was well informed and well connected. She knew some people in the embassy and the UN.

'Ghazala.. *Kem che*?' Shahida was obviously very nervous. 'Listen, stay indoors. Lock all the doors and windows. Nothing will happen. But there are rumours that some Lebanese and Indian supermarkets have been looted in the city centre. And one of the embassies has been burnt. Turn on CNN; they have a ticker reporting the latest developments.'

Shahida sounded breathless on the phone; obviously she hadn't seen anything like this in her home in Bombay. Shahida never forgave her husband for bringing her to Africa; she missed the energy of Bombay, the local trains and her family. She hated the days that she spent in Kinshasa. But, thank god for her English medium education; she found a job as an English teacher in an Indian school that kept her busy, and she formed a special friendship with Ghazala. She kept her sanity. Shahida often ordered *samosa, theplas, chevdo* and *biryani* from Ghazala's kitchen. Her hands concocted magic in the kitchen and most people preferred ordering traditional Gujarati *farsan* from her, as it reminded them of their mother's, aunt's or grandma's cooking. The kitchen income helped her send the kids to an International school, make friends and stay connected with different communities in the city.

Hetal sat quietly in the guest bedroom, reading her bible. Strangely her children slept peacefully through all this. Hetal could watch the unsuspecting Ghazala.

Ghazala switched to CNN, the ticker was on and the situation looked grim. All she could do was pray. And then there was a reckless knock on her kitchen door, Ghazala froze. 'Have the rebels reached my house? No!' She shuddered.

'*Ya khuda! Meher meher.* Not again,' she prayed. But the banging got more impatient. Her heart was pounding; she could hear the incessant, loud beats. The crack on the door revealed a familiar figure. It was Nawaz! Panting for breath, she stealthily slid open the door; it creaked eerily, while she opened it. And there he was, standing tall. She could see the bulge of his throat moving up and down, his lower lips trembling as his breathing got harder. She could see the hair on his chest sticking out from under his white linen shirt. He was leaning against the wall of the kitchen, eyes shut, fists clenched, and muttering expletives in French.

'They will never let this fucking country progress. *Tamey khabar che ney...* They are bloody looting all over. I was by my restaurant, offloading the supply from the pick up, when the motherfuckers got around. I did manage to escape, but the pickup is gone,' Nawaz rattled breathlessly.

'I ran for my life and saw your house and there was no other option but to seek your help.' He flashed his perfect smile, strong pearly white teeth; his eyes danced with the same naughty glint. He wiped the drops of sweat with the back of his palm.

Nawaz, ran the most popular Indian restaurant in town. All the 'happening' expats hung out there for their daily fix of exotic curries and chunky *tandooris*. He was extremely charming with a slow languid smile; lean and well-built body; a glass of gin and tonic; and a local cigarette hanging from his hand, which was his signature. Girls often vied for his attention; most wanted to visit the nightclubs with him, post-midnight, once he closed his restaurant. At 39, he was still single and people often wondered if he was a closet gay. When asked he would often laugh it off, saying a girl broke his heart and cooking is his only catharsis now.

Nawaz and Ghazala grew up together in Mombasa, they exchanged their first kiss in the meandering streets, and held each other tight whenever they could steal moments together. They explored each other's bodies till Ghazala's evil grandmother caught them together. Then all hell broke loose; her father slapped her hard and locked her in the room. Frantic calls were made to different extended families in Gujarat, to find a suitable boy for her; to get her married and done with.

Nawaz mustered the courage to ask for her hand in marriage, but Ghazala's father dismissed him, saying that they were proud Shias and would never marry the daughter to a half-caste Sunni. He was willing to run away with her. But petite Ghazala, couldn't muster enough courage to elope against her father's wishes and bring a bad name to the family. She married the *pucca* Gujarati guy, from Kutch, who her distant uncle had suggested.

A strange coincidence – here they were both in Congo, Ghazala married with three children and Nawaz, a suave restaurateur.

There he was in flesh! Ghazala's hands were pulled, as if by magic to the tiny trickle of blood meandering down his well-chiselled jaw line. She felt his green morning stubble.

'It's *haram*,' she reminded herself.

'*Khuda*! Why is he staring at her like that? Stop! Please stop!' She couldn't handle his intense gaze. Suddenly, she was conscious of her own crumpled cotton *shalwar kameez*. She could have dressed better. Oh! But how could she know that HE would turn up, and like this. Her hand went for her *dupatta*, there was no one at home that morning so she had taken off her hijab. Her beautiful firm breasts heaved along with her heavy breath.

'They remind me of a perfect, almost ripe papaya from Mombasa,' whispered Nawaaz, flashing his perfect smile. He wouldn't take his eyes off her.

'Nawaz, you are hurt. I will come back with some Dettol for you.' She rushed towards the living room. He leaned over and grabbed her arm.

'I can do with some alcohol right now, if you have some. I'm already intoxicated by those big watery eyes you have,' he whispered.

'*Yeh jheel see neeli aankhein koi raaz hai inmey gehra*,' he hummed, as he grabbed both her arms, towering way over her small frame. He looked down into her big eyes with that intense 'kill me now' burning gaze.

'No, not at this moment. The city is being ravaged by the rebels and here appears my former lover ravaging my body with his eyes.' Ghazala trembled. A strange electric current went down her spine. Every inch of her flesh was burning hot, throbbing with desire. She was wet down there. Her body craved this Adonis of a man. Why did she never experience this in years?

'It's *haram*!' she reminded herself again, and sent a silent prayer; but, all she could see was Nawaz's rippling muscles under his rolled up sleeves.

Ghazala opened the cupboard in the kitchen, and pulled out two glasses. All this involved too much energy. Her body refused to listen. The cells conspired against her will. The senses wanted him. They wanted to feel Nawaz. She whipped her tongue around her very dry lips. Her nether regions were pouring the divine liquid. She poured some Gin in the glass, while he was devouring every second of her body moves.

'Nawaz, I don't have tonic. Sprite... *cava*?'

'*Mais, oui! Madame!* I can see that you speak French,' he grinned.

'And you? Messing around with all the *besharam* white girls?' Ghazala hissed, with jealousy. Nawaz grabbed the bottle from her and gulped a stiff one, ignoring the chilled can of sprite on the kitchen counter. She fixed herself a strong potion and shot it down in one go. Both wouldn't let go of each other's gaze. Eyes transfixed, fire burning, too many questions to be asked, endless gaps to be filled in.

The moment was broken by the sound of a huge explosion, and Ghazala rushed into his arms. He held her tight. The two bodies entwined together and their breathing got irregular. More gunshots. Ghazala buried her head in his armpits. He smelled of cigarettes, gin and a hint of an old musky perfume. 'Boom, boom, boom'... more gunshots.

'Nawaz, do you think the rebels will take over? What will happen now?' squeaked Ghazala, choking on her own suppressed tears. Nawaz looked possessed. He had this long suppressed fire ignited again, burning in his eyes, and he held her delicate face between his huge palms and started kissing her. How fragile she appeared next to his own giant frame. He desperately wanted her.

Ghazala did try to push him away, but she felt a divine power was pushing her tongue into his mouth. He tasted sweet; she explored the inside of his mouth. Time stood still and both forgot to breathe. Her longest kiss in all these years. His mouth was an ocean of pleasure, a cave of strange satisfaction. She wanted to claim every cavity. He tastes sweet. What did he eat? A chocolate perhaps. Did a white woman gift it to him? She was jealous, outraged.

God, his body felt so good. The familiar comfort of his arms, she almost disappearing in that cosmic embrace. His hand found their way to her *shalwar* and he undid the belt one after the other dexterously, savouring every moment. Ghazala crumpled in his arms. The city could burn today! She didn't care. All she craved now was his manhood deep inside her. She was overflowing with desire and her breasts were swollen, hurting and waiting to be crushed by his hand. The *shalwar* fell on the ground, exposing her shapely legs. He shoved his finger into her, and she was wet. He slowly licked his finger after exploring her.

'You taste so good,' he wouldn't let go of her gaze. Ghazala closed her eyes and arched her petite body. Narrow waist, big butt and those luscious breasts; time hadn't changed her. Her body couldn't take all the electricity.

Another bomb went off, and the numerous Kalashnikov toting rebels shot randomly in Kinshasa. Here another body was being ravaged, violated by a rebel. Ghazala suddenly felt one with the city, as it crumbled bit by bit, burnt and was being overtaken by the rebel soldiers... here she was being consumed by her lover, Nawaz.

He ripped off her *kurta* and out popped her beautiful firm breasts, the big nipples standing erect. Nawaz rolled his tongue around it. A shiver went down her spine. She let out a moan. Her body was thrusting back and forth and she had absolutely no control, she was a woman possessed. He traced her body with his tongue, taking in every part. He kissed the little black mole on her waist bone.

She was naked, exposed, and vulnerable in front of him; just like the city was in front of the rebel soldiers. But the one big difference – she wanted him! He ran his finger down the hairline from her navel, to the nether region and suddenly he stopped.

She let out a scream, 'Noooo, don't stop! I want you down there. I want to feel you inside me.' Did she notice an evil grin on that most perfect face? He licked the trickle of sweat drops coming down from her breast to the navel, she lifted her body offering herself and he slid his hand under her, kneading her big, protruding, firm butt.

Nawaz took off his belt, undid the buttons of his powder blue, torn-at-knees jeans, and stepped out – all in a fraction of a second. She took off his white linen shirt. He was gorgeous inside. She clawed him and he let out a cry, full of agony. 'Bitch! Don't stop!' She bit his nipples, explored his vast expanse of chest with her clever and crafty tongue, and kept spitting out the hair from his chest. He grabbed her by the hair and pinned her down to the kitchen floor.

The glass windows shook with the exploding bombs around town, the doors rattled, the kitchen floor was vibrating, and Nawaz and Ghazala were consumed by their own private volcano. It was waiting to erupt. He was on top of her. Her beautiful voluptuous body right under him, the big breasts panting. His mouth was on her breasts and he finally entered her. Big, swollen and throbbing.

'Nawaaaaaaz,' she cried out. *Boom, boom, boom,* more gun shots and shattering of glass somewhere. She was wet, overflowing and Nawaz moved in and out of her.

He was crushing her breasts and then he asked 'Did you ever think of me?'

'All the time, Nawaz. All the time,' she hissed. He slapped her hard, right across her face. She was stunned.

'This is for not eloping with me in Mombasa.'

'Nawaz I was young and you did nothing for a living. How in the world could I?' Ghazala whispered, tears brimming in her eyes.

'Now don't cry. You know, I can't handle your tears.' He entered her again, harder thrusts and he moved up and down swearing at her for betraying his love. She gyrated her hips back and forth in tandem. Tears streaming down her cheeks. It was beyond her control. This is the best sex ever, she wanted more of him, she is married woman, the children are stuck in the school, her breasts are melting in his hands, the phone is ringing, it could be her husband, she has a million little nerves playing havoc inside her, and there is a huge explosion inside her... She arched up... collapsed again... She grabbed his hair, pulled him down and kissed him full on, while he kept rocking inside her. Another very loud "Bang", a building blew up in the vicinity and Nawaz came inside her, releasing his pent up lava deep inside her. The yin and yang merged as one in Ghazala. They lay there in perfect embrace, while the city burnt outside.

Hetal sat absolutely still. The bible in her hand was shaking. Tears rolled down her cheeks. Her children miraculously slept through all this. She prayed for Ghazala, for she needed it.

A lot of damage was done to the country, but Seth Manikchand was made. He had achieved his dream of becoming a millionaire.

Boss... Live Life Kingsize

'Tonight Manikchand Seth will show the world who is the real "Boss" of Kinshasa. The gods are conspiring to help. Is it voodoo? The Juju is working in my favour?' Manikchand experienced a strange chill down his spine.

'No, motherfucker, go away. I'm strong. I don't need such thoughts.' He opened a cold bottle of Evian and took a few sips. His body quivered, but he could not control his nefarious thoughts. A sense of *déjà vu*. He closed his eyes and took a deep breath. There was a blinding white light and he saw a flash of police, prison and a splash of blood. He just couldn't close his eyes. He would close his eyes and all he would see was a splash of blood. His whole body shuddered. 'Maybe a puff of strong and pure *Afghani Ganja*, and I will be fine.'

'Tonight is my coronation. I will be crowned the King of Kinshasa. The real *Badshah*. Self-made and solid. People will talk about me and the grandeur of my party for years to come. I will serve more alcohol than they have ever seen in their lives. What did they say back in India? *Haan*, "*paani ke tarah sharaab*". Expensive alcohol will flow like water. And the surprise of the *soiree*?' He giggled and clapped.

'I have to remember to check everyone's reactions and expressions. The accented English speaking bastards. Doing *aaiyashi* with *baap ka paisa*. I will teach them how to be an *aiyash* with your own *paisa*. I am a self-made man, and unlike them I haven't inherited a fortune.' His new Blackberry phone was ringing ... '*ek baar aaja aaja aaja*'. He had this ringtone saved for Hetal, his wife.

'*Saali*, always calling me at the wrong moment. She always calls me to come back home. Like I have no other job but to listen to her *bakwaas*. Stupid Hetal.' He was irritated.

'*Ara ra … su che*?' he yelled into the phone.

'No, I can't come home for dinner. No, I said. I don't want to eat *dal dhokli* for dinner. I want mutton biryani!' He giggled.

'*Sui ja ab* and yes, tell all the children I love them.' Ramesh had a total of nine children with his wife. And with the local women, he lost count.

'Who cares?' he laughed.

Hetal obviously wasn't invited for tonight's party, for Manikchand had other exciting plans. He would make a grand entry escorted by a beautiful young girl. She was new and not yet part of the nightclub circuit. He paid her a monthly salary and she serviced him well.

'Tonight will be her debut. Let the world realise that I don't accept leftovers anymore. I create! She has not been touched by ten other men. But I can pass her on. They can enjoy the women I have used. *Aha* I am the Boss!' he thought.

'But before the big evening, I have to go and meet the old Juju. There is something about him. People swear by his ability to conjure up devils, kill the enemies and help acquire wealth.'

'It is difficult to get a rendezvous with him, but for me? Manikchand Seth, the old Juju is always available. It is true that I struck gold after I made the first animal sacrifice, and drank the blood on the insistence of the Juju.' Manikchand's head was throbbing with new and exciting ideas. There was a lot that he wanted to do. He was a determined man. A man on a mission.

'Its dollars, dollars and dollars, all the way. I love the feel of crisp dollars on my fingertips. It's like caressing the firm breasts of a virgin. Ahh, better than an orgasm. The intoxicating smell and the smooth feel. I can keep stroking it and get aroused. Then I take the bills to my coffers, just like I would take a virgin to bed,' Manikchand Seth laughed.

Manikchand jumped into his Range Rover and switched on the music system. It played his favourite Bollywood number…'*Dhinka chika, dhinka chika, eh, eh, eh … dhinka chika… barah mahiney mein barah tarikey se.*'

'Salman *bhai*, you are my Guru… what style man! And so many women! Ha, ha, ha,' laughed Ramesh.

'Eh, did it make a screeching sound? *Pappa*! We have to change the sound system and please get some French music that young people listen to,' he leaned forward and told his driver.

'You know, all my girlfriends? They are under twenty and love music, pizza and beer. All these young girls, *kamaal che*! Why don't they listen to Hindi songs? I can't understand English songs, what do they mumble jumble? *Behenchod*! How will I ever understand what they sing in French! *Saala*! *Magajmar.*'

He began to sing again, '*dhinka chika, dhinka chika, eh, eh, eh.*'

Manikchand and the driver were en route to the old quarters of the city, to meet the toothless old Juju.

'I have to meet the voodoo man before the party begins. Money is never enough and I want more!' The drive was long and meandering through the narrow, dark alleys. They crossed many tin roofed huts, *maquis* selling *brochette*, and make shift nightclubs.

'I love the African spirit. These people know the real meaning of life. They know how to be happy. Sing, dance and look good! *Saali*, my foolish wife. Ha! She has no dress sense. She roams around in one long *kaftaan* all day. Running after her children and trying to feed them. Come and eat. Come and eat. I hear "eat" so many times at home that I bloody can't eat at home now. She doesn't even look sexy. I mean, look at other wives, sexy like hell. Dressed in frocks like *pucca* British *mems*. My dick goes twang up, and I want to screw their heads out. But what to do, I smile at their lucky husband and very politely greet them "*Namaste Bhabhi*", and I think of their tight, tight cunts under their frocks. Do they wear nice sexy panties inside? So many women together showing off their legs, arms and breasts. There have been times when I wanted to reach out and touch their breasts.' His brain never stopped thinking.

'It's all Hetal's fault. At heart, she is still that woman from her village. *Arre*, change a little bit *bhai*... Be modern *shodern*. But, *nahi*. She insists on being a *behenji*, forget dressing up, she doesn't even colour her hair. And now, this new drama with the church. Who attends religious meetings in church and forgets their own normal life? She doesn't deserve a cool dude like me!' he thought.

He looked at himself in the rear view mirror, unshaven, unkempt, stained teeth, salt and pepper hair and a big scar across his cheek. His finger caressed it, the deep scar running from his jaw line towards his left ear. Deep, dark and deathly. He was almost killed by the knife fight he had in the jail in Kandla port, Gujarat.

'I am such a *harami*, I survived. Nobody can get me... Shoo... Gooo away... This is no time to think about my previous life.' He looked away from the mirror. 'Why can't I look into my own eyes in the mirror? Ramesh is long dead. Hello Seth Manikchand!' He looked out to distract himself from his thoughts. His gaze fell on the young girl shaking her booty to '*sava sava sava allez*' on the road next to a rickety bar. She was sipping Guinness and dancing.

He rolled down his power windows and yelled at the girl, '*Yaka Yaka,*' waving a five dollar bill. She ran up to him and snatched the money. Soon a bunch of *shegues* were banging on his car, asking for money.

'*Bhag saala! Kende, Kende,*' he yelled in Lingala.

His driver shooed them away and parked the SUV near a safe spot. He called out to two of the urchins, to guard the car.

He handed them a fiver and whispered, '*Attention*. Be alert! *Cava*?'

'*Oui monsieur. Nous sommes la.*' The driver winked and rushed to follow his master.

'It would be impossible to walk like this in my village in Gujarat. You know back then, my village was full of filth, garbage and shit. But you Africans are clean, brothers!' Manikchand laughed at his own joke, and his driver was walking right behind him. The old Juju was sitting outside his hut. He was drinking Guinness, while listening to some music on his phone.

'*Mon papa! Comme vas tu?*' greeted Manikchand, and they did their customary head bang (it's just like the three formal kisses on the cheeks instead its head to head three times).

'You bring me nice gift?' asked the old man.

'Ha! Ha! Ha! *Pappa* make me rich *rapide*. I give you many, many things and a young wife!' Manikchand handed him a bottle of Black Label, and whispered something in his ear.

The old man waved his hand and spoke in his typical raspy voice, 'You see all top musicians? They come to me. I make them rich and famous. Don't worry tonight I make a big sacrifice.' The old man went inside his house and came back with an amulet and tied it around Manikchand's neck.

'This will kill all the bad intention of your enemy and protect you from evils.' Manikchand paid him five crisp $100 notes and rushed to the SUV.

He planned to stop at Memling, the five star hotel in *Centre Ville*, take a bath there and then go for his party. The Kinshasa crowd would see that he had a room permanently reserved under his name at the hotel. He was trying to live just like the other rich people. There was that smile on his face that he couldn't hide.

'*Dhinka chika, dhina chika, eh, eh, eh...*' he sang along.

Manikchand whipped out his Blackberry and dialled a number listed as '*Cherie du jour*'.

'*Ma Cherie...* muwaaah, *gros, gros bisous. Oui j'taime... Beaucoup, beaucoup.* Did you pick up my suit from the dry cleaners? Ok, ok, *merci!*' He giggled at something she said.

'Listen, you don't sell my suit for small money. Can't trust your type of girls with anything. Kinshasa and its girls are not the same. They have become modern, can sell anything for personal profit. I'm reaching Memling. Get ready and keep my suit on the bed.' He knew he would look like his favourite Bollywood star, Salman Khan, tonight. His suit had come from Bombay. He had ordered a burgundy velvet jacket and black velvet pants, with a white satin shirt. Just like rich people wear in the serials aired on Zee TV.

'*Barah mahine mein, barah tarikey sey, main tujhse pyar jataoun ... dhinka chika, dhinka chika, eh, eh, eh...*' the song was stuck in his head, and he sang in the loop.

He jumped out of his SUV and sprinted towards his reserved suite in Hotel Memling. He kept staring at his latest Blackberry phone, but knew that all eyes were on him. '*Saala,* look at their envious faces. I will show them tonight.' His time had come.

Manikchand Seth would like to invite you for his Birthday Celebrations.

Venue: The Ballroom, Grand Hotel.

Attire: Black tie.

Cocktails begin at 8 p.m. followed by sit down dinner and surprise.

The invitations were already sent out a week ago. Upper class Kinshasa society was buzzing with rumours related to this party.

'He has called dancers from Brazil,' said one.

'Oh, he is a big showoff, an air bag, all faff no substance really. It will be a cheap striptease. I won't even attend,' said another.

'He has been harassing me to attend. I just might go briefly to show my face. But my wife has completely refused to attend. She can't stand his sight.' But, the truth was, everyone wanted an invitation to this party. They all wanted to attend.

The Grand Hotel parking was packed to its capacity with luxury cars. Guests were forced to park their cars on Avenue Tchatchi. It was a gathering of the "who's who of Kinshasa". Important guests were flown in from different cities of Congo. Guests clad in fancy gowns and black ties were escorted into the Ballroom by tall, slender, Victoria Secret-style-models of every skin colour. The crowd was awed by the elegant black and white décor of the Ballroom. Fresh white orchids on every table; personalised seating; and the bartenders were creating exotic cocktails at four different bar counters. Classy, elegant and regal. There was nothing tacky about it. *Madame* Simone, the French owner of *Le Mille Fleuer*. An event management company was in charge of food, décor and drinks. It was *Parisienne* Salon chic. White gloved waiters were walking around with mini *vol en vents*, delicate *canapes*, crab *farci* and other *petite amuse bouche*. Manikchand Seth was standing at the door, welcoming each guest personally. He was living his dreams.

Dinner was announced and the guests sat down at their assigned tables to sample the special French cuisine. The music was loud and lights psychedelic. Papa Wemba, the legendary Congolese musician ran in from a side entrance, singing his latest song. The crowd was ecstatic.

'Encore! Encore! Encore!' shouted the guests.

'*C'est pour mon frère*, boss Manikchand!' Papa Wemba sang another popular song. Manikchand was dancing next to Papa Wemba.

Manikchand grabbed the microphone and announced, '*Mesdames et Monsieur. S'il vous plait.* Put your hands together for Fally Ipupa.' Fally Ipupa, the latest singing sensation sang his new song, while the guests whistled and clapped.

Lights were dimmed, candles lit and champagne continued to flow. Suddenly there was a collective gasp, everyone was looking at the ceiling. Ten beautiful Indian girls were hanging on multi-coloured ropes from the ceiling. The music unfolded and the trapeze artists performed gravity defying stunts. The crowd cheered and clapped with every unique act.

The spotlight shifted to the centre of the hall. A stunning Bollywood dancer, dressed in sheer white and gold Indian attire, sat on the carpet. Red lips, big kohl lined eyes and glitter on her cheeks. Her slim body was adorned with bright gold jewellery. She sat there, eyes cast low, and head slightly bent at an angle, and tapped her toes gently to the beats of the music. The bronze balls on her anklet tinkled. She looked up, surveyed the crowed and gracefully twirled to the beats of the music. Four background dancers dressed in rich green traditional Indian outfits, joined in. This was a typical Bollywood '*Mujra* style' performance.

The dancers caressed a cheek here, or danced on the table-top there. They sat on the laps of few lucky gentlemen, and pulled in the guests to join them. The music reached a crescendo, the dancers started stripping; the guests were cheering hysterically. The dancers stripped to bare minimum, revealing crystal-studded red bikini suits. The grand finale was a fast paced cabaret performed on the bar tables. The guests were breathless from dancing and drinking. The party finished at 4 a.m. Kinshasa hadn't seen anything like this in the longest time. 'Cheers!' Manikchand popped another bottle of champagne for breakfast, as the guests staggered out.

He sipped the golden liquid in the silver flute, 'Love me or hate me but you can't ignore me.' He smiled.

Manikchand's Range Rover was waiting in the portico of the Grand Hotel. The valets rushed in to shut his door, as he sat. He rolled down the glass and handed out a crisp $100 note.

'Share it. I am very happy,' he told them. The valets clapped and cheered as the Range Rover drove away. The sun was rising against the Congo River horizon.

'It will be a new day,' thought Manikchand. He called up his entertainment Manager, Suraj Deshpande immediately.

'Suraj *bhai*. It was a *tabahi* night, I tell you it was too much. Top of the top entertainment. Keep it up.' Manikchand asked his driver to pick up the dancers from the African

Dreams hotel. He was taking them to Black River for a special picnic.

'Girls get ready for nice hot breakfast at the river. This is Congo and I am the King,' he yelled at them, as they were getting down from the mini van. They didn't get a chance to change their clothes or freshen up.

'Don't be formal with me. Get into the car fast,' he instructed. The girls had no other option, but to hop into his car. He sang Bollywood songs, clicked pictures enroute and regaled them with his repertoire of jokes. Manikchand had invited some important clients to have breakfast with the 'Girls' at Black River.

Manikchand had hired Suraj Deshpande some months ago to supervise his warehouse.

'You Bombay people enjoy too much, no?' asked Manikchand. 'Every night, new girl at the dance bar? Beer and babe in Bombay, free flowing,' he laughed.

'No, Boss. The government has closed all the dance bars in Bombay. Now the bar girls are out of job. They sometimes perform in private functions. It's not like before.' Suraj pretended to look sad.

'Eh, Suraj. I have an idea. Bring some bar girls here in Kinshasa. I will run a Bombay style dance bar. It will be something else, very classy and private bar. Top class men will come, you will see. All the women travel for two months in June. Our poor brothers look like orphans. I can't see them in that sad state. They need some entertainment while the wives are gone. Its social service, you see. You know how much I love charity. All the sophisticated English speaking types will come running. Suraj, arrange now, now. I can't wait.' Manikchand Seth laughed.

Soon Manikchand was operating a nameless dance bar out of a huge villa in the City Centre. One hall called *Mughal-*

e-Azam, was a huge favourite among the Indian and Pakistani community. Fresh white linen covered mattresses and bolsters were spread wall to wall. People sat on the floor like olden times to watch the *Mujra* dance performance. The men competed in giving tips to the dancer, to perform right in front of them. The *Moulin Rouge* room had a disco and bar atmosphere. Bombay Spice had private performances. Manikchand kept the security tight, privacy was guaranteed and no cameras were allowed in. This nameless joint was the most happening place. This was the new pilgrimage in Kinshasa. Manikchand was revelling in money. He had stopped counting now. He was the *Grande Patron*.

The entire town was talking about Manikchand's unprecedented rise, his money and his reckless lifestyle. Seth Manikchand didn't care about people's opinion of him. He was busy amassing wealth and enjoying all the luxuries money could buy. He could sniff money, and these days he was minting it.

Epilogue

3-1-2014
Avenue de Fleur, Gombe, Kinshasa.
Democratic Republic of Congo.
Time : 4:00 a.m.

Sameer emptied his fully loaded pistol into his father's chest. Bang, Bang, Bang… Every bullet sought revenge for the humiliation Sameer and his mother suffered… The bullets were not enough to punish Manikchand Seth, for he had gone beyond the code of humanity. His lust for money, power and women morphed him into a demon. Sameer was in an eye lock with his father.

'*Pour quoi*?' he mouthed. Manikchand smiled. He was defiant in death. Sameer was choking, he couldn't breathe. He fell on the velvet sofa and broke down. Manikchand Seth fell on the red and white, Chinese fur carpet. He was holding his chest. 'Call doctor,' he tried to whisper, but the words wouldn't leave his mouth. Blood was oozing out. The carpet was wet. Manikchand could see his entire life flash in front of his closed eyes…

Ramesh Patel, *aka* Manikchand worked in a local Indian company that exported timber out of Congo. He was just the right man, from dealing with port authorities to pesky police officials. He laughed and joked with everyone in the government office, calling them his brothers and brothers-in-law. They received gifts in cash and kind from him. And his work never was stopped in the bureaucratic rigmarole.

He was supervising the loading of timber on the banks of the Congo River and noticed all the useless scrap lying around including old containers, rail tracks, cabins and tanks. The port authority had no means or money to get rid of them, and the original owners had long dumped their waste here. The metal scrap was such a nuisance, occupying space that could be used for storing timber. But what to do with it?

'*Saala*, I am sitting on the diamond mine. This will be my new business. I will export scrap metal to India. They are littering the port here. So some *seva,* community service in English! I will rule the Congo River now,' he thought to himself.

'Congo River, broad and majestic. It flows down sometimes in rapids, sometimes calm, and divides the two capital cities, Kinshasa and Brazzaville. The only river in the world that slices the two capital cities, as if someone took a knife and tore Kinshasa and Brazzaville apart. But it nourishes and nurtures, providing livelihood to thousands of Congolese who carry on trade ferrying fish, vegetables, fruits, plastic, timber, imported cars and people on flat barges,' he was telling a Belgian investor.

'I will take you there myself,' he continued. 'It is a sight to behold, 20 to 30 Land Cruisers packed together on a flat wooden barge, floating down the majestic river. Local men gently row the barge down the river, protecting the expensive cars from dents and damage, screaming at passing speedboats that might topple the barge over. The rich people swish and swoosh up and down the river on their custom-made jet skis. The old money loves having fun on the Congo River. One can see revelry happening on little sand banks. People dock their speedboats on these islands and enjoy a good barbeque, surrounded by the beautiful river. The expats and rich locals frolic around, while their local staff arranges the picnic. From designer canopies to fancy barbeques, to the best hookah and white linen. Everything is carried and perfectly arranged. The waft of meat being grilled on the charcoal and gorgeous setting makes it just perfect. Sunday, you and I will go there for a picnic.' The Belgian investor looked interested.

'The big ships, however, dock on the river port where export containers are loaded and sent off to Matadi, the main port on the Atlantic Ocean,' he said.

'The Congo River is unbelievable. It has the energy of another level. The river port is bustling with prostitutes, policemen, beggars, flies, custom officials, vendors, onlookers, men and women engaged in animated discussion in French or Lingala. Huge *balloons* of second hand clothes, shoes, stuffed toys waiting to be cleared and sold in the local market. Plastic furniture and household goods. Fresh fish, spinach, yams, dried caterpillars, meat all await inspection and clearance.'

'You have to be strong. There is a perpetual unbearable stench of urine, dried meat, fish and sweat. Women hawkers dominate the river port. They sell bright coloured pines or African fabric, freshly grilled meat, bread and eggs, and water. The energy is palpable, and it's throbbing with people of all colours. This is the place where money is made. The place of employment and the place of intense corruption. It tests your patience, your wheeling-dealing abilities and your ability to manoeuvre out of the mad maze. And once the code is cracked, the palms greased, the custom officials release the goods. They are then ready to be sold. I am a master of all this, *mon frere*. You have met the right person. I will help you set up your business.'

Seth Manikchand could feel life escaping him. He was dreaming. He was dreaming of the Congo River port.

Wheel barrows full of frozen chicken from the Middle East, He can tell from the Arabic written on the plastic packaging. It's lying unattended and thawing under the sun, while the owner negotiates the price to get it out of the port.

The local protocol officer of the Arab importer is arguing with the custom official, 'Look at the produce, don't you realize it's frozen? And look at all the flies hovering over it. My *patron* has agreed to pay you a monthly sum if you allow his goods to pass hassle free. He might be new in this business but he knows the "Big" people here.'

'Big people!' laughed the custom official. 'Do you find any one of them here?' He spread his arms around. 'Do you see anyone of them here? They don't come here *mon ami*. It's us, who work under the sun without any salary. Don't waste my time,' barked the custom official. 'Go to the big people. They will come and release your chicken.' The protocol officer ran back to his Arab patron and whispered in his ears. Soon an agreement was reached and an amount paid. The frozen chicken, absolutely thawed now, was ready to be sold in the fancy *supermarche's*. They were quickly packed in the Nissan pickup, ready to be delivered to the stores.

An old Greek man, an importer of sundry goods was lusting after a young coquettish girl.

He yelled and asked her, 'Are you free for beer?'

'Yes, old man!' she giggled, 'but how much you pay?'

'I pay you beer, *poulet* and $10.'

She showed him her middle finger and said, 'Shove it up your ass.' The old man laughed.

'Why don't you come and help me do it?' the man asked.

'Last price for you, $50, ok?' It was finally settled at $25, and the young girl walked along with her companion for the afternoon.

Ramesh laughed a deep throaty laugh as the old Belgian man walked away, holding hands with the young girl. She was swinging her hips, as some of the men gaped at her with lust and desire. He was sitting on the steps of his office; actually a container that was converted into a basic office with a fitted AC, a table and a few chairs. The heat inside was unbearable. His red polyester shirt and khaki pants were sticking to his body. The old AC whizzed providing the comforting sound of something running, but not the much needed respite from the oppressive heat. He picked up a sheaf of papers to fan himself. The papers were actually a summon from the *parquet* (local court). He understood enough French to know that it stated that he was involved in some illegal activity, and their business will be closed immediately.

'This country will never progress if these good-for-nothing officials continue to extract money like this.' He was angry.

He flashed his latest Nokia phone from Dubai and called a court official, '*Bonjour, mon frère.* You want us here in business or we go? Who will pay you if we stop operating? Didn't I send you $500 last week? So what does this notice mean? I will not pay a single *franc* now. Do what you want to.' And he disconnected. He watched, his eyes scanning the container, were the people around him impressed? Did they realise that he was the real boss! He controlled everything, the police, the government and the port.

Ramesh stepped out of the container, and one of his men ran to put a plastic chair for him to plonk on, while another carried his phone. He loved being powerful, it gave him vicarious pleasure. That intense feeling to show the fucked up Kinshasa society that he had arrived.

'Nathalie, *ma cherie donne moi ma cigarette,*' he pouted. Nathalie, his latest squeeze was all of 16 years old, actually she was younger than his son. She had come to his office asking for a job. He hired her as his personal assistant. He always ordered take away pizza, for her entire family of six. He paid her well. She would sit on his lap, and button and unbutton his shirt when his old friends came visiting.

Laughing, cooing and purring, she was his most prized pet *du jour*. His Indian friends would squirm and look away when she kissed him right on the mouth, while he was in the middle of some discussion with them. He loved their discomfiture. '*Saala*. Happily married and lusting after my girl.'

Manikchand Seth lost his final battle with life. Sameer sat there crying, 'Why? Papa, why?'